THE
THIEVES
OF
PUDDING
LANE

This edition published 2014 by
A & C Black, an imprint of Bloomsbury Publishing Plc
50 Bedford Square, London, WC1B 3DP
www.bloomsbury.com
Bloomsbury is a registered trademark of Bloomsbury Publishing Plc

ISBN 978-1-4729-0318-1

A CIP catalogue for this book is available from the British Library.

Printed and bound by CPI Group (UK) Ltd, Croydon CR0 4YY

1 3 5 7 9 10 8 6 4 2

THE
THIEVES
OF
PUDDING
LANE

JONATHAN EYERS

A & C BLACK
AN IMPRINT OF BLOOMSBURY
LONDON NEW DELHI NEW YORK SYDNEY

Prologue

February, 1666

'Wake up, Samuel. Come on, son. Wake up.'

Samuel only opened his eyes as far as a squint. Yellow candlelight gleamed off his father's face, leaning over his own.

'What time is it?' Samuel asked, his throat dry. All he felt like doing was going back to sleep.

'Time to get up,' his father said quietly. Then he pulled back Samuel's woollen blanket.

Samuel sat up as the winter chill surrounded him. He clutched his arms to protect them from the cold draught, then buried his hands in his armpits. Looking across the bed chamber, he couldn't even see the first hint of morning light shining through the crack between the shutters. It was still the middle of the night.

'What's going on?' he asked, suddenly worried.

'Get dressed, Samuel,' his father said. 'Quickly.'

On the other side of the room Samuel's older brother was kneeling over his chamber pot. When he finished he stood up and shed his crumpled nightgown. Glancing round, he caught Samuel's eye. Thomas looked just as confused, and just as worried, as Samuel felt.

'Come on, boys,' their father insisted. 'Do as I tell you, please.'

Samuel swung his legs over the side of the bed and started pulling off his nightgown too.

His father went over to the large oak chest both brothers shared. Placing the candle on the floor beside it, he lifted open the lid and began to pull out clothes. He already had a couple of half-filled canvas sacks lying on the rug. As he pulled out clothes he stuffed them into one of the two sacks, making sure he filled them about the same.

'I have sent word to Father Stephen,' he told them, glancing back at Thomas to make sure he especially was listening. 'He is expecting you. Go straight to St Clement's church. He will do what he can for both of you.'

Samuel saw his brother nod unquestioningly.

They both dressed quickly after that. Samuel's still-tired fingers fumbled with the buttons of his grey tunic. Then he tugged the same black breeches he had worn yesterday up his legs. They were cold on his skin, and Samuel shivered. Lastly he slipped his freezing toes into his hard wooden clogs and stretched his legs.

When the brothers had finished dressing their father held out the sacks. 'One for each of you,' he said. 'There's fresh bread at the bottom of both. Now, be very quiet coming down the stairs. I don't want you to wake your mother.'

Samuel and Thomas took a sack each and followed their father down the narrow wooden steps. Samuel made sure to avoid the third from the top, which he knew creaked.

'I want to say goodbye to Mother,' he said.

'Quietly, Samuel,' his father whispered. 'She's asleep.'

But as they reached the bottom of the stairs Samuel heard the loud sneeze from her bed chamber, followed by a sticky, hacking cough, then another sneeze that sounded full of spit.

'She's awake now,' Samuel said.

'There's no time now, you have to go,' his father said, not trying to be quiet any more. 'Father Stephen is expecting you.'

Then he clamped a forceful hand over Samuel's shoulder and guided him to the front door. Samuel allowed himself to be led without any more argument. Thomas went willingly. At the door they stopped long enough to don their worsted coats.

Their father opened the door. Samuel stepped out into the frosty night first. It had snowed again, but not heavily. A fresh layer of pure white covered patches of dirty snow beneath. Taking his first breath of frozen air got rid of the last bit of tiredness that kept trying to drag Samuel back into his dreams. He sighed out a billowing cloud of visible breath.

'You're the oldest,' his father whispered into Thomas's ear, but Samuel still heard. 'You have to look after your brother. Promise me that. Don't let him come back here. Don't let him out of your sight for a moment.'

'I promise,' Thomas whispered back.

'And take this.'

Samuel saw his father press a few coins into Thomas's hand then squeeze the older boy's fingers tightly over the top of them.

Their father didn't say anything more after that. The smile he gave them looked far too cheerful, thought Samuel. After a moment, he shut the door between them.

Samuel heard the key turn in the lock.

Thomas grabbed Samuel's wrist tightly. 'Come on,' he said. He had suddenly adopted an authoritative tone, as if he was pretending to be their father. 'You heard what he said.'

After a moment Samuel didn't need to be pulled along. He trotted beside his brother, trying to keep up with him. Together they headed down the narrow lane towards the church, their clogs clacking noisily on the cobbles as they went. Samuel glanced back only once, but the house had already vanished into the shadows of a moonless night.

Thomas kept his word to his father and didn't let Samuel out of his sight for the rest of the night, which they spent at St Clement's with Father Stephen. He didn't let Samuel out of his sight all of the next day either. Father Stephen took them to one of his neighbours, who had agreed to let them stay for a while.

But Samuel still wanted to see his mother and, unlike his brother, he hadn't made any promises to their father.

Samuel waited until Thomas fell asleep the next night. They had been given a pile of blankets on the floor of the parlour. It wasn't as nice as a bed, of course, but Thomas was so tired he started to snore within a minute of lying down. Samuel watched him sleep a little longer, wanting his brother to be in a deep sleep from which he wouldn't be easily woken when Samuel got up.

Thinking himself rather clever, Samuel didn't put on his clogs until he got out into the street. He padded barefoot out of the parlour and stood in the dark hallway as he pulled his outdoor clothes on over the nightgown his father had stuffed into his sack. Then he opened the front door slowly, and shut it again with even greater care. He and Thomas had gone to bed early but the owner of the house might still be awake, he thought.

The freezing ground bit at Samuel's feet and he quickly pulled on his clogs. He kept to patches of snow as he headed down the street, the snow's softness cushioning his footsteps and allowing him to walk quietly past the parlour window.

It was another dark, moonless night and the streets were empty again. Samuel hadn't gone far before he realised this was the first time he had been out on his own after dark. By the time he got home he was running.

But when he reached the front door he stopped instantly. He didn't knock. He didn't move at all. He didn't even breathe. He couldn't.

Two brutal strokes of red were painted on the front door, slashed one across the other in the sign of the cross. Dribbles of paint had bled down the rough-hewn oak where it had been applied thickest. Samuel didn't need to touch it to see it was still wet.

He and his brother had seen this sign on enough doors in the past year to know what it meant. Plague. But he had never expected to see it on this front door.

As he stood there, frozen to the spot, the dull sound of a heavy bell being slowly rung came around the corner. When Samuel finally turned his head and looked he heard the clattering of cart wheels on the cobbles. A straining, snorting horse loomed out of the darkness, pulling the cart, and led by a man in black clothes. The man rang his bell again.

Samuel stepped back, under the jettied upper storey of the house opposite, where he hoped the shadows would make him invisible.

As the cart went past, its wheels cutting ruts through the slushy snow, Samuel saw the large dirty canvas. It rose in the middle where it covered whatever was piled in the back of the cart.

Only after the cart had passed him by did Samuel see the bare foot with a grubby sole sticking out from beneath the canvas.

He started running then, away from the cart, away from home, but he couldn't run far enough fast enough to escape the bellman's shrill words.

'Bring out your dead.'

Chapter 1

Several months later

Samuel had lost count of the number of times he walked past the costermonger's stall. Perhaps five or six by now. It was never busy enough, so he kept on going.

The butcher's stall next to it, on the other hand, was always busy. A crowd of people jostled to see what the thickset bald man in the bloody leather apron had for sale. A constant fog of buzzing flies bothered the air overhead, probably drawn by the same rich, juicy smells of fresh meat that made Samuel's hungry belly rumble with thoughts of steaming roast beef, turnips and carrots. When the butcher wasn't cleaving great chunks of red meat with loud thuds he used his heavy-looking battered iron knife to swat at the flies.

Samuel heard the cook before he saw her, and realised his opportunity had finally come.

The cook was a small, thin woman whose neck seemed to be swallowed by the many bulky layers of her clothes. Her dun-coloured overskirt was pinned up at the back. She wore a white bonnet and white gloves, and the two girls that she kept berating in a piercing voice were dressed to match. They all had well-scrubbed ruddy faces, and each carried a wicker basket over her left arm.

After the butcher wrapped several pieces of meat in waxpaper and the cook dropped the package into one of the girl's baskets, the three of them moved on to the costermonger.

Samuel's heart began to thump in his chest, and his belly tightened with trepidation. At least the fear and the excitement stopped him feeling so ravenously hungry. Glimpsing the clock on the church steeple towering over the marketplace he realised it was now exactly one whole day since he had last had so much as a scrap of bread to eat.

As luck would have it, another couple of women stopped at the stall to check out the costermonger's cabbages at the same time. Samuel held his breath as he squeezed in, trying to make it look like he was just perusing too.

The cook had immediately started using her piercing voice on the old, bent-backed costermonger, whose flickering eyes looked out from under the wide brim of his hat. She was keeping him distracted, Samuel thought. Good.

Slowly, careful not to touch anyone, he reached a hand out behind her back. His fingers settled on the cool, smooth skin of the apple.

Samuel had spied this particular apple on his very first time walking around the marketplace. It was the one nearest the front of the stall. It looked bruised, as if it had rolled off onto the cobbles more than once, but Samuel was so hungry he suspected it would still be the sweetest, juiciest apple he had ever eaten.

As he withdrew his arm, the fruit felt so big. His hand felt so small. He tucked his free hand into the other armpit, ready to hide the apple beneath his bent elbow.

He had thought the only eyes watching him belonged to the dead duck hanging upside down from the rail above the butcher's stall. He was wrong.

'Thief!'

The girl's voice was just as piercing as the cook's. Samuel shot her a shocked look. She hadn't been paying attention to the cook. She had seen everything.

He broke into a run. Not fast enough.

'Got him!' a man's angry voice growled.

But the hand at Samuel's throat had missed his neck. Samuel felt the rough fingers claw the skin over his spine. Then they grabbed hold of his tunic instead.

Already mid-run, Samuel jerked back in the man's grip. The front of his tunic rode straight up his neck and cut in under his chin. He choked. His hands flailed open. The apple fell. Gone.

'I'll horsewhip you, boy!' the man hissed.

Fear sliced down Samuel's back like the lashes of his unseen captor's whip. He struggled and squirmed, preventing the man from grabbing him with both hands. Everyone was looking at him. He knew he had to escape quickly, or he wouldn't escape at all.

Just then Samuel's tunic ripped with a sharp tearing sound. Still resisting the man's pull, Samuel suddenly felt loose. He was free.

His feet were already moving.

'Thief!' The man's shout echoed the girl's.

Samuel aimed for the shrinking gap between two large, converging groups of people heading in opposite directions across the marketplace. He ran full pelt, so fast he worried he might trip over, but he didn't dare slow down. The man was chasing him, and he was faster than Samuel.

Faces turned at further shouts of 'Thief!' and 'Stop him!' and people glanced at Samuel as he ran past, but it took them too long to realise the darting boy was the guilty one.

Samuel scouted out for city watchmen. If some of them joined the chase, he knew he stood no chance of escaping.

Suddenly the crowd became thinner. Too late, Samuel realised his fatal mistake. By running toward the midden heap, the pile of dumped dung and discarded rotting vegetables at the edge of the marketplace, he was going where most people tried to avoid.

The man pursuing him was closing in.

'Hide in the alley behind the church,' a boy's voice said behind him.

Samuel briefly turned his head as he ran, expecting to see whoever had said it running beside or behind him, but there was nobody there.

Samuel kept going, chest and legs burning with fear and with the exertion, his ripped tunic flapping as he went, but he quickly realised the man's heavy boots had stopped thundering after him. Not slowing, Samuel quickly glanced back over his shoulder again. A scruffy boy with dirty, matted fair hair and clothes too small for his gangly body stood in the man's way, hands out, begging.

Samuel looked back again when he reached the lich gate of the churchyard, just in time to see the man grab the boy by his narrow shoulders and shove him out of the way.

Samuel ducked through the open gates and hid himself behind the thick wooden gatepost. If he ran now his only route was through the open churchyard. If the man was still chasing him then he would see Samuel run.

Samuel didn't dare move. He stood there, back pressed against the gatepost, arms in front of him, trying to make himself as small and as narrow as he could. He listened, but heard only his own heart thumping wildly.

Then he heard the man's feet again. They slowed as they approached the churchyard. He was right outside. This was it, Samuel thought. If the man came in, Samuel knew it would all be over. Holding his breath, he could already feel on his back the bite of the flogging he would get. But there were punishments worse than a flogging.

Eventually the panting man swore, then grunted to himself. Listening hard, eyes pressed tightly shut, Samuel heard the man's clogs on the cobbles. They were slow, at walking pace, and getting quieter, further away.

Samuel finally allowed himself to breathe an enormous sigh of relief, bent over, hands on his knees. For a moment he thought he might be sick.

The worst thing, he thought, now it was all over with, was that he had been branded a thief for nothing. All those people had looked at him and seen only a criminal who deserved to be punished. Meanwhile Samuel had only got to hold that apple for a few seconds. He was now absolutely convinced it was the juiciest, sweetest apple he'd never get to eat.

His belly rumbling so loudly he could hear it, Samuel snaked his way between the gravestones and left the churchyard by the back alley.

'There you are,' said a loud voice.

Startled, Samuel almost staggered back through the lich gate, to the delighted guffaw of the voice's owner. Fortunately it wasn't the man who had been chasing him.

'You're the one that helped me,' Samuel said.

The skinny boy with messy hair stopped sniggering. 'Help you?' he said indignantly. 'I reckons I just saved your life, thief.'

The word was cutting. 'Yes, I suppose you did,' Samuel admitted. 'Thank you.' He moved slowly towards the boy and held out his hand. 'My name's Samuel.'

'Though I reckons you're the worst thief I ever saw,' the boy went on, ignoring Samuel's hand and keeping his own behind his back.

'I do all right,' Samuel lied. He shrugged. 'It was just bad luck I got caught this time.'

The boy grinned. Samuel knew he didn't believe a word of it.

'The first mistake you made was only stealin' an apple. An apple! That don't fill your belly. Even if you'd got it and eated it, you would've been hungry again in an hour, 'specially if you ain't eated anything since yesterday. Which by the looks of you, you ain't.'

He was older than Samuel. Samuel had to look up to look him in the eye. The sleeves of the boy's brown tunic didn't reach his wrists and his tatty grey breeches didn't cover his knobby knees. His hair stuck out at different lengths all over his head, as if he had cut it himself.

'The second mistake you made,' the boy continued unabated, 'was hangin' around that stall in the market like an annoyin' fly. People who are goin' to buy something don't hang around, they just buy something. You looked like a thief. An' a bad one at that.'

The truth hurt. 'Well, I didn't see you there,' Samuel said defensively. 'If you're such a great thief, why did you wait until I got caught? Why didn't you help me earlier?'

'Catch.' The boy only gave Samuel a second's warning before he stopped hiding his hands behind his back and tossed something high into the air.

Samuel reached out to catch it before he saw what it was. He felt the cold hard lump fall into his cupped palms and then saw the ripe sheen of the apple's skin. The boy produced another apple from behind his back and took a big, loud crunching bite out of it.

'This is the one I dropped,' Samuel said. He was sure of it. He had stared longingly at its bumps and bruises when it was sitting on the stall. 'The one I stole.'

'No,' the boy said, mouth still full. 'That's the one *I* stole.' He finished chewing, swallowed with a satisfying gulp, then smiled a grin of gappy teeth, some of them broken, most of them black. 'Me name's Wilf. And of course you didn't see me in the market. Because, like you said, I am a great thief. Now, eat it.'

Samuel didn't need to be told twice. He opened his mouth and bit deep. Juices squirted into the corners of his mouth and some dribbled down his chin. It was indeed the sweetest, juiciest apple he had ever tasted.

He was so hungry he almost forgot Wilf was there. Samuel ate down to the apple's core but then nibbled that too, spitting out any pips he sucked up. Wilf ate his apple more slowly, watching Samuel all the time and smiling to himself.

When he finished, Samuel let out a little pop of a burp and grinned. He tossed the stringy remnants of the apple core into the dusty gutter.

'Bread,' said Wilf. His tone was friendlier now. 'That's what you should try and steal. Go for the little loaves. Bread fills you up better than apples.'

Samuel nodded, more open now to the other boy's wisdom. 'Can you show me?'

Wilf's blue eyes flashed brightly as the sun appeared from behind a cloud. 'I think you need to come 'nd meet Uncle Jack.'

Chapter 2

'He's got a wooden leg, but don't ever let him catch you lookin' at it. Look him right in the eye or don't look at him at all. Just so you know, it's his left one he's missin'.'

Samuel listened mostly in silence, nodding occasionally to show he was paying attention, as Wilf told him about this man he called his uncle.

They walked as Wilf talked. Samuel didn't know where Wilf was leading him, but he knew this part of the city reasonably well. People, carts and horses bustled along Cannon Street in the direction of the Tower. Samuel and Wilf wove in and out between slow hooded wagons, fishermen carrying stinking baskets of freshly caught eels over their shoulders, and goats and pigs being herded to market and protesting very noisily.

'He used to be in the Royal Navy, see,' Wilf continued. 'He got his foot blown off during a sea battle. A cannonball got blasted into his ship right next to where he was standin'. He got a face full of big wooden splinters too. Lucky to be alive, really. But then the ship's doctor had to saw off the rest of his leg, right up to the knee, because it was so badly injured. An' the sea battle was still ragin' all around 'em when he did it!'

Samuel thought Wilf sounded in awe of the man. But Wilf was right, this uncle of his was certainly lucky to be alive. Samuel didn't get a chance to agree before Wilf started talking again.

'After that he became a smuggler. I heard the middle of his wooden leg is hollow. There's just an empty space there, big enough to hide stolen jewels. He wrapped 'em up in a cloth so they didn't rattle around. I've never seen it meself, of course, but I reckons it's true. I think he might have been a pirate. I asked him once. Don't make that mistake!'

'Why?'

Wilf shook his head and lowered his voice. 'He just looked at me with a glare that chilled me to me toes. He didn't say anythin' for what seemed like a really long time, then he just said, "Don't ask." And then he laughed.'

Wilf turned onto Pudding Lane, a narrow winding street of old wooden houses whose upper storeys projected out overhead. A woman was leaning out of one upstairs window, hanging washing on a line strung across the street. As Samuel and Wilf walked underneath, the shutters of the house opposite opened and another woman leant out to do the same. The two women started chatting. Despite being on opposite sides of the street, they were close enough to shake hands.

'Where are we going?' Samuel asked, not for the first time.

'The Three Sisters. Not far now. It's just down here.'

Near the bottom of the lane Wilf took Samuel into a small cobbled courtyard behind the houses. It smelt very badly of horses, muck and hay. On the other side of the courtyard were stables, but the horses were not there. Someone had tried to sweep up the dung but had ended up just brushing it further across the cobbles. Wilf nimbly picked his way around the chunkiest deposits and Samuel tried to follow in his footsteps.

Wilf stopped outside the inn. Samuel thought the crooked building looked abandoned, its shutters closed, with cracks in the grey unwashed walls.

An unsettling loud croak drew Samuel's attention upwards. He thought it was a crow perched on the roof at first, but then he saw it came from the old wooden sign hanging outside the inn. The sign creaked again as the breeze tried to swing it on its rusty hinges. Though the paint was flaking, Samuel could see it showed three women. With hunched backs and chins longer than their noses they looked like witches, he thought.

Wilf put his hand on Samuel's shoulder. 'Before we go in,' he said in a quiet voice, 'you need to know that you should always, always call him "Uncle Jack".'

Samuel frowned. 'But he's not my uncle.'

'He's not my uncle either.'

'Whose uncle is he, then?'

'I don't know. But that's what he wants to be called, so that's what we calls 'im.'

Wilf pushed the heavy door open. It wasn't as stiff as the sign, but it still let out an awful juddering creak that Samuel felt gnaw at his bones. It let out another as Samuel pushed the door shut again behind them.

The heat and darkness inside the Three Sisters swallowed Samuel instantly. Having just left bright sunshine, his eyes took a few moments to grow accustomed to the dim, flickering yellow glow from the candles in the middle of the tables. As well as daylight, the closed shutters kept out fresh air. Stale, pungent smoke swirled around Samuel as he followed Wilf toward the bar. The inn was almost empty, but when Samuel coughed quietly into his hand, several men stopped muttering into their clay flagons and looked round.

Samuel kept his eyes on Wilf's clogs, pretending he hadn't even glanced at the dark figures hunched over the tables. The men soon went back to drinking their ale and smoking their pipes.

'Evenin', Mr Boyle,' Wilf said cheerfully to the man behind the bar. 'Is Uncle Jack here?'

The barman, Mr Boyle, was a tall and rather fat man with a bumpy bald head that reminded Samuel of a potato. He looked Samuel up and down as he arranged empty flagons at the front of the bar, but his stubbly face remained expressionless. 'Back any time,' was all he said.

Wilf nodded. 'Let's sit down.' He gestured to a table in the corner, away from everyone else. Samuel would have chosen the same one.

When he sat down he found it very rickety. He rested his arms on it and the tabletop wobbled, making the pool of candlelight spill wildly for a couple of seconds. His chair also had loose fittings. Samuel sat completely still, staring between Wilf and the wall behind him. He started to wonder if coming with this strange boy had been a good idea after all.

Wilf opened his mouth as if to start talking, but then the door creaked open again. He looked past Samuel. Slowly, Samuel turned to look himself.

Framed by the daylight streaming through the doorway was the dark shape of a big man wearing a long flowing coat and a large hat, his weight noticeably shifted to one side, where he supported himself with a stick.

'That's him,' Wilf whispered, as if Samuel hadn't guessed already.

After the door creaked shut behind Uncle Jack the entire inn was silent. Only when he began making his way toward the bar did the muttering start up again, but quieter than before.

Samuel watched Uncle Jack get closer. The shadow of Uncle Jack's wide-brimmed hat cast a shadow over his face, so Samuel couldn't see where he was looking, whether he was looking right back at Samuel. Wilf made a move to get up. His chair scraped against the floor. The front of Uncle Jack's hat jerked in their direction.

Uncle Jack was looking right at them. Then he was coming towards them. Samuel held his breath.

But before Uncle Jack reached them, another man got to his feet. He had been sitting alone at one of the other tables without a drink. He stepped into Uncle Jack's path, shoulders hunched anxiously and head bowed, clutching his hat in front of his chest. Uncle Jack stopped and stood up straight to regard the man, towering over him.

Samuel got his first glimpse of Uncle Jack's face then, and his wide, angry-looking eyes.

The man said something to Uncle Jack that Samuel couldn't hear, and Uncle Jack motioned to an empty table in the other corner with his gloved hand.

Wilf sat down with an impatient sigh. 'Don't stare,' he told Samuel in another whisper.

'I'm not,' Samuel whispered back.

The truth was, he couldn't help but stare. He watched the man sit down opposite Uncle Jack and start making big apologetic gestures, palms up and open, arms spread wide. Samuel didn't see Uncle Jack say anything. The dim light from the candle shone on his pressed lips, his set jaw.

Eventually the man took something out of his pocket and put it on the table. Samuel didn't see what it was, but Uncle Jack leaned forward and put his gloved hands over it. When he waved a hand to dismiss the man, whatever had been on the table was gone.

The man scurried out of the inn. Slowly, Uncle Jack removed his gloves. Samuel felt as though his heart had jumped out of his chest when Uncle Jack lifted an arm in his and Wilf's direction and beckoned them with two cocked fingers.

'Come on,' said Wilf, getting up again.

As he and Samuel reached the table, Uncle Jack finally took off his hat. Samuel found himself looking into a long face lined with several deep dark scars. He could see the whites of Uncle Jack's eyes, which made him look fierce, even when a pleasant smile spread across his thin lips.

'Sit,' he told both boys. He had a deep, smooth voice. He flattened his long silvery grey hair where it had been unsettled by his hat.

'I've found you a new magpie, Uncle Jack,' Wilf said.

'Yes, I see,' Uncle Jack said, not taking his eyes off Samuel. 'What's your name, lad?'

'Samuel.' He tried to sound fearless.

'Are you an orphan?'

Samuel nodded.

'Plague?'

'Yes.'

'Any brothers or sisters?'

'I had a brother. Thomas. But he got sick too.' Samuel found these questions easier to answer than he usually did, when anyone bothered to ask, perhaps because Uncle Jack asked them so quickly. So many people had lost family and friends to the Plague that Samuel had long given up expecting any sort of special sympathy anyway.

'Where do you live?'

'Well, until a short while ago, Father Stephen at St Clement's was looking out for me. But he has a lot of younger children who need his help now, so I couldn't stay at—'

'Do you live on the streets?' Uncle Jack interrupted.

'Yes.'

Uncle Jack lifted his head, looking at Samuel down his long nose. 'Are you a thief, Samuel?'

For the first time Samuel hesitated. It was bad enough being called a thief by someone else without calling himself one. It wasn't as if he had stolen much, just a few pieces of fruit. Most of the time he ate other people's thrown-away scraps, but even they didn't seem so abundant anymore. He knew he would have to get a new woollen coat from somewhere somehow before next winter, though. As it was, he was still wearing the clothes he had left home in.

'Did you hear me?' Uncle Jack asked.

'Yes,' Samuel said quickly. 'I am a thief.'

Uncle Jack nodded and sat back. 'I don't know how much Wilf here has told you about my little magpies. When you meet the rest of them you'll find they all have similar stories to tell. They're all Plague orphans, just like you. None of them have any family left, no one to look after them. I do what I can, but I am not a rich man.' His mouth opened in a wide crooked grin. Many of his teeth were black like Wilf's. 'And if I help you, then I expect you to help me.'

'Of course.' Samuel nodded eagerly.

He listened quietly, still nodding, as Uncle Jack explained that he would let Samuel sleep in the cellar below the inn, that he would provide Samuel with a straw mattress to sleep on, and that he would give Samuel something to eat both morning and night. Samuel's belly began to rumble again at the thought of food. His hunger made him ready to agree to anything Uncle Jack said.

'In return for a roof over your head and food for your belly,' Uncle Jack continued, 'you will give me as much as you can get. You don't even have to steal it, if you don't want. You can beg for it, if you fancy, see how much that gets you. But if you do steal, whatever you do, don't get caught. If you get caught thieving, that's your concern, not mine. If they want to flog you or hang you for it, you only have yourself to blame. Understand?'

Samuel nodded again. The thought of the hangman's noose made the breath catch in his throat but another rumble from his belly drowned out any apprehension.

'So what do you say, Sam?' Uncle Jack said, loud all of a sudden. 'Do you want to be one of my little magpies?'

'Yes, very much so,' Samuel said swiftly. He knew by now Uncle Jack had no patience for hesitation.

Uncle Jack nodded once more and glanced over at Wilf for the first time in several minutes. 'Good. Wilf here will take you under his wing for the next couple of days, teach you a thing or two.'

'I'll teach you a thing or two,' Wilf echoed.

'Thank you,' Samuel said, to both of them.

'Now, I can hear your stomachs from this side of the table,' Uncle Jack said. 'How about some supper, you two?'

Burbling again, Samuel's belly answered for him.

Chapter 3

Samuel followed Uncle Jack and Wilf behind the bar, past the unblinking stare of Mr Boyle, and down the dusty stone steps that led into the cellar below. Before they reached the bottom Samuel heard other boys' voices chattering noisily and boisterously. They sounded older than him, their voices deeper, like Wilf's.

When he entered the cavernous cellar Samuel saw the three boys halfway across the room, lighting candles from an oil lamp. The cellar was much bigger than the inn above it. Samuel realised it extended under the courtyard quite a way.

The boys were placing the candles on top of oak barrels. The barrels filled the cellar. They were lined up at this end of the cellar but stacked all the way up to the low ceiling at the other. The boys didn't hear Uncle Jack arrive because they were being too loud but when they spotted him they came over, quickly winding their way through the maze of gaps between the barrels.

'Who's this?' one of them said, cocking his head toward Samuel.

'I'm Samuel.'

'And you're going to be nice to him,' Uncle Jack added.

'I always am, aren't I?' The boy smiled at Samuel, but the smile vanished the instant Uncle Jack wasn't looking at him any more.

As they spoke more boys started to appear, but not from the steps behind the bar. A shaft of orange sunlight cut through the dusty gloom at the far end of the cellar. Samuel saw more steps leading up to a wooden hatch at street level. The boys came down, some of them on their own, others in pairs or groups of three.

'Where's Mr Morley?' said a short boy, younger than Samuel. 'I'm starvin'!'

'Finish lighting these candles,' Uncle Jack told them. 'Nobody eats in the dark.' Then he turned round and headed back up the steps into the inn.

'Grab some candles,' Wilf told Samuel.

Samuel queued up to light the wicks of the greasy-feeling candles from the oil lamp, then followed Wilf into the dark unlit corners. Wilf moved expertly through the cellar, ducking his head beneath the wooden beams that supported the low ceiling. After scraping his own head against one and getting cobwebs in his hair, Samuel realised he would be ducking a lot himself.

'Make sure it doesn't fall over,' Wilf said, showing him how to stand a candle up by grinding the bottom until the soft wax splayed out.

Samuel noticed some of the boys watching him, but none of them introduced themselves, and Wilf didn't introduce him to any of them either. They had lowered their voices now, no longer noisy or boisterous, and he couldn't hear anything they said any more. He guessed that meant they were probably talking about him.

'Can I have some food?' Samuel asked. His hands were starting to feel weak and shaky.

'Not everyone's here yet.'

'How many magpies does Uncle Jack have?' he wondered aloud.

There were more than a dozen boys in the cellar already, too many for Samuel to count at a glance. The air had quickly filled with the smell of dirty bodies and unwashed clothes, combined with the smell of burnt fat given off by the candles. Samuel began to feel hot. It was stuffy down here, even more so than in the inn above.

Samuel was planting more candles and looking around for that straw mattress Uncle Jack had promised him when someone else appeared from the hatchway, trotting quietly down the steps. Samuel thought it was a small boy at first, younger than him. Then he realised it wasn't a boy at all. With her hair hidden beneath a big, shapeless woollen hat, and her face just as dirty as all the others', the girl probably got mistaken for a boy quite a lot.

She caught him looking at her and gave him a nervous little smile. It was the only sign of friendliness Samuel had encountered since coming down into the cellar, so he smiled back.

'What's her name?' he asked Wilf.

Before Wilf got a chance to answer a raucous cheer went up at the other end of the room. Samuel turned. Uncle Jack was back. He was cradling a stack of wooden bowls in one hand, enough for everyone. The boys rushed forward to grab one of them before he dropped any.

'Come on,' said Wilf, blowing out his last candle.

Samuel was so hungry he smelt the food before he saw it. Waiting behind the little girl and Wilf, he took one of the last few bowls. Inside, the battered bowl was stained black, but Samuel didn't care. It represented the promise of something to fill it, and then fill his belly.

At that moment two men came down the steps. One of them was Mr Boyle. Samuel had never seen the other one before.

'That's Mr Morley,' Wilf whispered, as if it was a terrible secret.

He made a little gesture toward the man, who was taller even than Uncle Jack. He was thin with a nose like a chicken's beak, long and pointed. He wore a wig

34

of tight raven-coloured curls, just like the King's, and a long deerskin coat. As he stopped beside Uncle Jack, Mr Morley's small eyes swept over the boys in the cellar with a contemptuous look. Samuel noticed he carried a square of black slate, and tucked under his arm was a small wooden chest.

Mr Boyle, meanwhile, was struggling to carry a large charred pot by himself. Samuel saw the steam billowing out from its bubbling contents.

'Line up and fill your bowls,' Mr Morley ordered.

Everyone obeyed him, forming a line that stretched back into the cellar. Samuel was content to be at the back of the queue, even though he felt famished.

But what happened next, he found very odd. Everyone ahead of him filled their bowls, as Mr Morley had instructed, but not with food. They emptied pockets and pouches and hiding places in their clothes into the bowls. Samuel saw the little girl put a few coins and a gold earring into hers. Wilf dropped a small handful of clinking coins into his.

'I don't have anything,' Samuel whispered into Wilf's ear.

'You don't need anything,' Wilf whispered back. After a moment he added, 'Today.'

One by one those ahead of Samuel filed forward. When Wilf got to the front Uncle Jack emptied his bowl into the wooden chest and said something to Mr Morley.

Mr Morley scratched something on his piece of slate with a stub of white chalk. Then Uncle Jack handed the bowl back to Wilf. Now Samuel was at the front.

'Sam has just joined us,' Uncle Jack explained to Mr Morley, who gave Samuel a cold look.

'Anyone else?' Mr Morley said.

'No, that's it.'

For the first time the rowdy boys were utterly silent. Samuel saw they were all watching Mr Morley intently. His lips moved without speaking as he worked something out on the slate. Samuel didn't know what everyone else was waiting for, but their apprehension was infectious. He found himself holding his breath too.

Then Mr Morley said, 'Robert.'

Both the girl and Wilf looked relieved, and they weren't the only ones. Samuel looked over the others' faces for the one boy who didn't seem as relieved.

'Close the hatch behind you,' Uncle Jack said.

The older boy who had smiled at Samuel and made an unconvincing promise to be nice had an angry scowl on his face. He ducked his head and shuffled away to the steps at the far end of the cellar. He elbowed Samuel out of the way as he pushed past him.

'Where's he going?' Samuel asked Wilf.

'Eat well and sleep well,' Uncle Jack said. 'Tomorrow is another day.'

Then he turned and went back upstairs again. Mr Morley snapped the wooden chest shut, glared at Samuel, then followed Uncle Jack up the steps.

'One at a time, boys, one at a time,' Mr Boyle said impatiently.

A couple of the bigger boys hefted the steaming pot onto the top of a barrel. Mr Boyle stood behind it, rolling his brown-stained sleeves up his fat and hairy arms. After wiping a bare forearm across his shiny, sweaty forehead he waved an old wooden ladle in the air and laughed huskily. Then he began slopping the food into the bowls.

Eventually Samuel reached the front, by which time he was almost ready to eat one of his own fingers. Mr Boyle had to scrape the ladle around the bottom of the pot to fill Samuel's bowl with what looked like lumps of mushy boiled potatoes in a milky soup. Samuel didn't care what was in it. It was food and it smelt lovely.

Five minutes later he was sitting cross-legged between the barrels with Wilf, his bowl empty but his belly full. He let out a little burp. Wilf laughed, but sudden hiccups cut his laugh short. Samuel laughed too. Neither of them had spoken as they ate, which made Samuel think Wilf had been just as hungry as Samuel had been himself.

Samuel spotted the little girl sitting alone on the other side of the cellar.

'What's her name?' he asked again.

'Catherine,' Wilf replied.

'We should let her come and sit with us.'

'No we shouldn't,' Wilf said sharply. 'You don't want to be friends with her. She can't teach you nothing. She's a terrible thief, almost as bad as you. I reckons she'd steal from us if she could get away with it. Let her sit on her own.'

Suddenly one of the boys burst into song. He had a terrible singing voice, flat and croaky, but after a few words others began to join in, including Wilf. Samuel had heard children singing this song on the streets but he had never really paid attention to the words. Soon he was the only one not singing, but by the last chorus he remembered enough of it to join in too. For the first time everyone was looking at him with smiles instead of wary stares.

The singing continued into the evening, and when they finally ran out of songs Samuel felt tired, as though he'd been running instead of singing.

In the sudden quiet Samuel heard how busy the inn had got since supper. People were singing up there too, their slurred voices barely muffled by the ceiling. Heavy footfalls clopped across the floor of the inn in time to the music. When people danced above his head Samuel saw little wisps of unsettled dust sink down from the ceiling.

Some of the boys appeared with what looked like large grey canvas sacks.

Wilf leapt up. 'Come on. You've got to be quick or you end up with a dirty one.'

He took Samuel to the space behind the barrels where the sacks were stuffed. As Wilf shook one out and laid it on the floor, Samuel realised these were the straw mattresses Uncle Jack had promised. They all seemed dirty to Samuel, marked with old stains and smelling of a dusty floor, but as he fluffed his up and placed it beside Wilf's, Samuel told himself at least to be glad he didn't get the one with straw spilling out of a tear in the side.

Sitting down on it, he found it to be a lot more comfortable than he expected. It wasn't a bed, but it was much, much better than some of the places where he had slept in the last few weeks. The soft patch of overgrown grass in the churchyard where he had spent the previous night had felt like hard stone when he woke up this morning.

A couple of boys blew out the candles nearest them.

'Do we have to go to sleep now?' Samuel asked.

'We can talk until the candles burn down if we want,' Wilf said.

Samuel saw the candle on the nearest barrel had melted to little more than a waxy mound with a burning wick sticking out of the top.

'But we have to be up at dawn if we want to eat,' Wilf went on. 'So we prob'ly should go to sleep now, I s'pose.'

He stood up. Samuel thought he was going to blow out the candles but instead he stepped nimbly over Samuel.

'I'll be right back,' he said.

'Where are you going?' Samuel said, starting to get up. 'I'll come with you.'

Wilf wrinkled his nose. 'I usually piss alone, Sam.'

Samuel felt himself blush. 'Oh.'

Wilf gave him a black grin, then disappeared up through the hatch at the far end.

Samuel pulled off his clogs and lay back on his straw bed, stretching his hands behind his head and wiggling his toes in the air as he waited for Wilf's return.

Only seconds after Wilf left, Samuel heard a shuffling noise approach, as though someone was trying to creep up on him. He sat up immediately.

Catherine crouched down in front of him, glancing at the others as if she didn't want to be seen talking to him. Then she glanced up at the hatch Wilf had just vanished through. 'I'm Catherine,' she whispered, holding out her small hand. She wore fingerless woollen gloves.

'I know. I'm Samuel,' he whispered back. He shook her hand. 'What's wrong?'

'He'll be back any moment,' she went on. 'I just wanted to warn you before he comes back.'

'Warn me about what?'

'Wilf.'

'What about him?'

'You can't trust him.' She shook her head and looked Samuel straight in the eye. She had large brown eyes and beneath the grime, Samuel thought, an honest face.

Before he could ask her what she meant, Wilf reappeared, still buttoning up the front of his breeches as he came down the steps. When he saw Catherine he noticeably quickened his pace. Catherine slipped back to her own mattress before Wilf reached them.

'What did she want?' he demanded.

'Nothing. Just making me feel welcome.'

Wilf let out a little snort then he blew out the candles and settled down to sleep.

'Goodnight, Wilf,' Samuel said.

Wilf just grunted.

One by one the rest of the candles in the cellar went out, either blown out or reaching the ends of their wicks. In the darkness the sounds from the inn above seemed further away.

Samuel lay staring into the blackness for a while, wondering why the boy Mr Morley had called Robert never came back. As weariness dragged Samuel into sleep he also pictured Catherine's earnest face when she told him not to trust Wilf.

It would be another couple of days before Samuel found out what she meant.

Chapter 4

For the first time in weeks Samuel slept through the night and didn't wake up once. Not that he had time to appreciate it when Wilf poked him awake at dawn and told him to put his clogs on, and quickly, if he wanted any breakfast.

Samuel barely had time to finish the thick, chunky gruel a sleepy, red-eyed Mr Boyle ladled into his bowl. Wilf gulped down his bowlful without stopping and then leapt up again.

'Come on!' he urged Samuel impatiently.

By the time Samuel saw the black bottom of his bowl most of the other magpies had already left the cellar.

Coming up through the hatchway into the courtyard, Samuel squinted painfully against the bright sunlight. He was used to seeing the sunrise. Sleeping outside he had tended to wake when the city rose from its slumber, when people began to fill the streets, and their voices to fill the air. It was never a good idea to be found asleep in a sheltered shop doorway when the shopkeeper arrived to open up for the day.

'So, what are you going to teach me today?' Samuel asked Wilf.

Wilf stuck his nose in the air and announced, 'How to pick pockets.'

'An essential skill for any young gentleman!'

Wilf nodded and grinned.

They left the courtyard and Wilf led the way to Gracechurch Street, turning onto Lombard Street. Samuel imagined there would be plenty of pockets to pick around here, where the richest people in the city lived in three- or four-storey townhouses with lead roofs and windows that actually had glass in them. But Wilf kept going.

Samuel guessed where to as they cut through to Cornhill.

'In the mornings there's always plenty to be got at the Royal Exchange,' Wilf explained. 'Every thief in London knows that, and every rich man in London knows every thief in London knows that too, so you got to be clever.'

'Just tell me what to do and I'll do it,' said Samuel.

'All in good time, all in good time.'

The Royal Exchange stood like an ancient stone temple on an island where several streets converged. Samuel had never seen Cornhill anything other than busy, whether it was late at night or early morning like this. People flooded through the crowded streets around the Exchange as though the roads were rivers and the people were caught in the current.

Samuel was surprised when Wilf suddenly stopped and said, 'Here.' They were still quite a way from the row of pillars at the entrance to the grand shopping arcade.

'This is far too open,' Samuel said, shaking his head. 'We should go inside the Exchange. It's more crowded. People have to walk slowly, and stop often.'

Wilf gave him an indignant scowl. 'I thought I was the one teachin' you, not the other way round. Of course, if you don't need me help…' He trailed off.

'Sorry,' said Samuel sheepishly. 'I just thought we might get more if we went inside.'

Wilf's scowl turned into a wicked grin. 'Trust me, Sam.'

Samuel couldn't help but recall what Catherine had said the night before.

Wilf explained what they were going to do.

'Half of stealin' is gettin' away with it,' he said. 'An' the quicker you do it, the more likely you are to get away with it. Stand there with your hand in someone's pocket for more than a second and you will get caught.'

Samuel remembered his apple yesterday.

'In and out, quick as possible,' Wilf went on, making a jabbing gesture at Samuel's ribs. 'And the easiest way of doin' that is knowin' where they've got their money before you try.'

'How do you work out where they keep it?'

'You keeps your eyes open, and then you makes them show you.'

'How?'

'Here, give me your foot.'

Before Samuel knew what was happening Wilf had grabbed Samuel's ankle and was pulling his leg up behind him. Samuel had to hold onto the wall of the map shop they had stopped in front of to keep his balance. Then Wilf let go of his foot again.

Turning round to ask why, Samuel received a faceful of Wilf's fingers. 'Hey, what are you doing?' he cried.

'You look too clean.' Wilf smeared something rough and gritty on Samuel's cheeks.

Samuel realised the roughness and grittiness came from the bottom of his clog.

'There,' Wilf said, smiling almost proudly at what he had done. 'Now you look like a proper urchin and someone might take pity on you. Sit down on the cobbles here, stick out your hands and try an' look like you're really sad an' hungry.'

Saying no more, and not giving Samuel time to ask any questions, Wilf turned, headed up the street and didn't stop until he was almost out of sight.

Feeling dirty and itchy, but not wanting to scratch and unsettle Wilf's handiwork, Samuel sat down cross-legged on the cobbles and held out his cupped hands, just as Wilf had told him to. He didn't need to try very hard to look unhappy. He already felt ashamed of himself, and they hadn't even stolen anything yet.

He sat there for quite a while, completely ignored. Glancing along the street he caught sight of Wilf's impatient glare. He had to try harder. He stuck out his bottom lip, making it look like he might cry at any moment.

A man wearing a ruffled white shirt and a lace cravat slowed down in front of Samuel. He reached into the right-hand pocket of his black velvet breeches and pressed a farthing into Samuel's outstretched hands.

'Thank you, sir,' Samuel said, as surprised as he was grateful.

The man smiled through his wispy pointed beard then continued on his way.

Samuel suddenly realised what the man had shown Wilf.

In the time between the man slowing down and walking away again, Wilf had caught up with him. Wilf didn't even glance at Samuel as he strolled past. To everyone else, it wouldn't have looked like Wilf was following the man. Samuel watched them both go out of sight.

A short while later Wilf returned.

'How much did you get?' Samuel asked keenly.

'Doubled our money,' he said, showing Samuel another farthing.

Samuel laughed, but only briefly. A thought had occurred to him, a thought that might never have surfaced had he gone without breakfast this morning. 'It feels a bit wrong, though.'

'What does?' Wilf snapped.

'Well, you just stole from someone who was generous enough to give us something in the first place.'

Wilf snorted with laughter. '"Generous enough"? Let me tell you somethin' about these people, Sam. They live in mansions. They have servants who do everythin' for them. Do you think any of them has ever gone to bed hungry?'

Samuel shrugged, but he doubted it.

'No, of course they haven't,' Wilf fumed. 'They have so much money they don't need to make no more, but they still do anyways. They could lose half of it and still be dirty, stinkin' rich. But how much did that man give you? I'll tell you what he gave you, because I've done this enough times to know. It was the smallest coin in his pocket.'

Samuel nodded slowly. What Wilf said made sense.

'Right, get up,' said Wilf. 'It's your turn.'

Samuel's heart began to beat faster as he stood up. He still wasn't sure what he was doing.

Wilf sat down in his place. 'Go along there and do what I did.'

Samuel went along Cornhill and stopped where Wilf had stopped. Then he waited and watched, but took a grimace from Wilf to mean he was watching too intently. So he pretended to be looking for someone instead.

'Alms for an orphan, sir,' he heard Wilf say in a plaintive voice.

Just as when Samuel had been sitting at the roadside, most people ignored Wilf, some changed direction slightly to avoid him, and one or two gave the boy mean, even disgusted looks. Every time he saw someone do that he remembered what Wilf told him about mansions and servants and felt a little bit angrier, a little bit less ashamed.

Finally a large man with a thin moustache like the King's and who walked with a rolling gait stopped to fish a coin out of his pocket for Wilf.

Samuel stepped out into the crowd and strolled slowly in the direction the man was going. He matched the man's pace, keeping right behind him in the crowd.

Samuel had to make himself breathe. His heart was beating so fast he was worried the man might hear him gasp for air. As the crowd in front of the Royal Exchange got heavier, and progress slower, Samuel focused on that pocket. It had looked gaping when the man stuck his hand into it, but now Samuel was flexing his fingers, ready to make his move, the pocket seemed to have inexplicably shrunk.

Suddenly the man stopped. A horse and cart were causing a loggerhead on the street.

This was his chance, and probably his only one. Samuel slipped his hand into that pocket.

His fingers parted the material of the man's baggy breeches. Then he felt a fingernail scrape against something hard. The knots in his belly tightened with both fear and excitement. Wilf's words echoed in his ears: 'In and out, quick as possible.' Knowing he couldn't make a fist to grab the coin, Samuel gripped the cold metal between two fingers. Then he slowly withdrew his hand.

The whole thing had only taken a second, but Samuel felt like he had been standing there with his hand in the man's pocket for minutes.

As he turned, he realised nobody had been watching, nobody had seen him. Everyone was more concerned about the horse and cart blocking their way.

Samuel slipped sideways between two people, clenching his prize in his hand.

When he got back to Wilf and opened his fist, Samuel couldn't believe the coin that sat in the middle of his palm, glistening with sweat. He hadn't dared look at what he had stolen until now. All of the fear drained out of Samuel instantly. He felt giddy with excitement. He wanted to get back out into the crowd and have another go right away.

Wilf snorted when he saw the coin. 'Beginner's luck,' he muttered.

Samuel grinned to himself. After all, his shiny silver shilling was worth almost fifty times as much as Wilf's battered little farthing.

Chapter 5

After that it became something of a contest. Wilf's pride had clearly been hurt, because he insisted on having two turns in a row after bringing back only a halfpenny on the first go. The next time he came back with a couple of farthings and a stormy look on his face.

Samuel decided it probably wasn't a good idea to try and compete with Wilf, so he was content with whatever he managed to get. Wilf seemed almost pleased the time Samuel came back empty-handed. Perhaps he had been right about beginner's luck.

Just before noon, when the hot sun settled overhead and shrank all the shadows, Wilf abandoned his pickpocketing attempts and hurried back to Samuel. Samuel quickly saw why. Coming back from the Royal Exchange was an irate man with a billowing wig of curly blond hair that flapped around his shoulders like beagle ears as he stomped through the crowd. He swung his walking stick and cursed at other beggars, most of who scurried out of his way.

Samuel recognised him immediately. He had given Samuel a farthing and then Wilf had helped himself to whatever else was left in the man's pocket.

Obviously the man had reached into his breeches to pay for something in the Royal Exchange and deduced what had happened.

'Let's stretch our legs,' Wilf suggested, barely slowing down as he passed Samuel.

Samuel was already scrabbling to his feet. 'I think it's time for some lunch.'

'An exc'lent suggestion, my friend.'

They disappeared into the flow of the crowd before their angry victim spotted them.

Wilf stole some bread from the marketplace where they had first met, less than a day before. It felt like he'd known Wilf a lot longer than that. As they walked past the costermonger's stall Samuel held a hand up to his face, pretending to shield his eyes from the sun. He was terrified of being recognised and having to run again.

They sat on the cobbles at the edge of the market and Wilf tore the brown loaf roughly in half, sending a shower of crumbs falling into his lap. Begging and thieving was hard work, and the sweet floury smell of the fresh bread made Samuel feel hungry again. However, now he had the food to satisfy his hunger.

Only for a few seconds did Samuel think about the fact that they could have actually bought the bread with some of the money they had stolen.

Wilf finished his half of the loaf, jumped up and dusted the crumbs off his breeches. 'Back to work,' he announced.

The coins in Samuel's pockets clinked together as he stood up. 'We'll have to be careful or someone might pick our pockets.'

Wilf, whose pockets were just the same, hissed with laughter.

They spent the rest of the afternoon begging and stealing around the marketplace.

When an orange dusk descended over the city and the crowd in the marketplace thinned out Wilf decided they had done enough for the day. But when they pooled their takings together in the courtyard behind the Three Sisters he didn't look so sure.

'It's a lot of money,' said Samuel. It certainly seemed like it.

'Should be enough,' Wilf mumbled, mostly to himself.

'Enough for what?'

Wilf didn't answer. He reached out with both hands and scooped all the money towards himself. 'Uncle

Jack knows I was showin' you hows it's done today,' he explained. 'I'll put all of this in my bowl and tell 'im you helped.' Samuel saw his prized shilling disappear under a tide of Wilf's farthings.

A couple of boys were already lighting candles when Samuel and Wilf descended the steps into the cellar. Most of the others arrived within a couple of minutes. Samuel spotted Robert, the older boy who had left before they ate last night and never returned. Robert also spotted Samuel. He looked him up and down briefly then cast his gaze away. Samuel felt dismissed.

Samuel looked for Catherine too, but she wasn't here yet. She arrived just as Uncle Jack appeared with Mr Morley and his chest. Samuel joined in the cheer. Catherine was panting too hard to celebrate. Obviously she had been running hard to get here in time. When she saw him looking at her she gave a little smile. She looked nervous, Samuel thought.

'Line up and fill your bowls,' Mr Morley ordered, as he had the night before.

Samuel queued to collect one of the bowls from Uncle Jack, though Wilf put everything they had got into his own. It didn't look so much now it wasn't spread out over the cobbles.

Samuel spied the contents of others' bowls. Robert had got more than the two of them put together. He didn't look so apprehensive tonight, Samuel noticed. Catherine, though, had much less than him and Wilf. He saw her nibbling on her bottom lip.

When Samuel and Wilf got to the front Mr Morley looked at Samuel's empty bowl then lowered his piece of slate and glared at Samuel.

'Wilf was showing me how to pick pockets today,' Samuel said quickly, feeling the urgent need to explain. 'His bowl is full of everything we both got.'

'But mostly me,' Wilf added.

Mr Morley glanced at Wilf's bowl, then said, 'I'd hardly call it full of anything.'

'Tomorrow you will have to fill your own bowl, Sam,' said Uncle Jack.

Samuel nodded. He'd worry about that tomorrow.

As Uncle Jack tallied up what was in Wilf's bowl and emptied it into the chest, Mr Boyle came down the stairs with tonight's dinner in the big charred pot. It smelt exactly the same as last night's too, but Samuel was hungry enough again not to care.

Everyone waited in silence, watching Mr Morley's lips move wordlessly.

'Catherine,' he said finally.

Samuel looked at her, confused. He didn't know quite what this meant. She didn't look back at him. She looked only at her clogs.

'Close the hatch behind you,' Uncle Jack told her, and to everyone else he repeated what he had said the previous night as well: 'Eat well and sleep well. Tomorrow is another day.'

Then he and Mr Morley disappeared upstairs with the chest.

'Food!' Wilf said, and the word quickly spread around the magpies like a chant.

'Consider yourselves lucky, boys,' Mr Boyle said, wielding his ladle like a magic wand. 'It's got cabbage in it tonight!'

But as the ravenous boys clustered around him with their bowls, Samuel saw Catherine turn away. She left her bowl on top of a barrel and started toward the hatchway.

'Where are you going?' he called after her.

She didn't respond.

'Don't worry about her,' said Wilf. 'Come an' get somethin' to eat.'

Samuel ignored him. 'Wait!' he cried, hurrying to catch up with her. 'Catherine!'

Beneath the hatchway she finally stopped ignoring him, turned on the steps and gave him a sad look. Then she glanced over his shoulder, as if distracted by the sight of the boys getting their dinner.

'Where are you going?' he asked again.

'Up there,' she said quietly.

'Why? Why don't you have something to eat first?'

She nodded sharply at the others. 'Ask Wilf.' She sounded bitter, Samuel thought.

With that she trotted up the steps as quickly as she could and banged the wooden hatch shut. It rattled in its frame.

Utterly confused by what was going on, Samuel rejoined the others. Mr Boyle was scraping around in the pot to fill Wilf's bowl.

'Why did Catherine leave?' Samuel asked.

'Because she had to.'

'Why?'

'Because those are the rules.'

'What rules?'

Wilf let out an impatient sigh. His bowl was full and he clearly wanted to go and empty it into his belly. 'The magpie who brings Uncle Jack the least doesn't get nothin' to eat and they can't sleep here either.'

Samuel couldn't quite believe what he was hearing. 'You never told me that was a rule. Uncle Jack never said anything about that either.'

Wilf shrugged. 'Them's the rules, anyway.'

Samuel remembered Robert leaving after Mr Morley called out his name. He remembered Mr Morley making the marks on the slate as he and Uncle Jack inspected the contents of everyone's bowls. What Wilf said suddenly made a horrible kind of sense.

'Can I go an' sit down now?' Wilf said huffily. 'I want to eat this before it gets cold.'

Samuel took a step back, then held out a hand to stop Wilf passing. 'Wait. The only reason you had more than her was because I helped you.'

Wilf shifted his position, as if getting ready for a fight. '"Help me"?' he said, anger rising in his voice. 'I was the one helpin' you! You forgotten that? If I hadn't been tryin' to teach you how to steal then I would have got a lot more than I did, and I would have got a lot more than her too. Now, I'm goin' to have me dinner, so move.'

Samuel let him pass. 'But it's not fair.'

Wilf didn't turn back as he said, 'I don't make the rules. It's Uncle Jack's rules. If you don't like them, don't eat his food and don't sleep in his cellar. It's your choice, Sam.'

Samuel wanted to leave. He wanted to throw his bowl against the wall, storm out of the cellar and find Catherine to tell her he had left the Three Sisters and he wasn't going back and he was proud he had stood up for her in the name of fairness.

And perhaps if Mr Boyle hadn't dropped a ladleful of food into his bowl at that moment, perhaps if Samuel hadn't already been holding his dinner, and perhaps if his empty belly hadn't immediately started rumbling, perhaps Samuel would have done those things.

Instead he went and sat down next to Wilf and started to eat.

'She knows the rules,' Wilf said through a mouthful of food. 'An' they didn't bother her when it was someone else who had to leave last night, did they?'

'I know,' Samuel said quietly.

His dinner didn't taste as nice tonight. Every time he swallowed some salty potato he imagined Catherine eating scraps she found on the street.

After dinner he didn't join in the singing. He received a dirty look from Robert for not taking part, but he didn't much care.

It took Samuel a long time to get to sleep that night. After all the candles had gone out he listened to the quiet snoring of the other boys curled up on their straw mattresses. He lay there with his eyes wide open, seeing only the blackness all around him, because when he closed his eyes he saw Catherine's face instead.

Chapter 6

Samuel awoke to the sound of the hatch being thrown open above his head. Opening his eyes a crack he saw the dawn sun shining brightly into the cellar. Having taken so long to get to sleep it took him a long time to wake up too. Only after he saw most of the boys clamber up into the courtyard did his weary brain realise Wilf hadn't woken him up.

Suddenly wide awake, his heart racing, Samuel sat upright. Not only was Wilf not asleep next to him, but his straw mattress had already been put away too.

Samuel leapt up and pulled on his clogs. He finally spotted Wilf. At first he thought Wilf was queuing for breakfast, but as he squeezed past the magpies heading the other way, he saw Wilf reach the front and add his dirty bowl to the pile of other dirty bowls next to the pot.

'That's your lot,' Mr Boyle said. When he carried the pot away he let it hang by his side, holding only one handle. There was nothing left to spill out.

'Wilf, why didn't you wake me?' Samuel demanded.

'Can I get past?' Wilf said coldly.

'Why didn't you wake me up in time for breakfast? I'm hungry.'

'I'm not your manservant, Samuel.'

Wilf followed the others. Samuel followed Wilf. 'I'll need to steal some bread,' Samuel told him.

'That's up to you,' said Wilf.

'I'd like some help.'

Wilf stopped at the bottom of the steps and turned back to him. 'Then ask one of the others. I did what I could yesterday. You heard what Uncle Jack said last night. Today you're on your own.'

'He didn't say we couldn't work together. He just said I had to fill my own bowl tonight.'

'Yes, an' so do I. Which means I can't waste me time tryin' to teach you how to steal.'

Samuel was still tired, and Wilf's unfriendliness was making him angry. 'But the only thing you taught me yesterday was how to work together.'

Wilf sighed. 'I don't 'ave time for this. You're a useless thief, Samuel, and I can't change that. I tried. But there's just no teachin' you.'

He didn't hang around to hear Samuel's response, but he would have had to wait a long time. Samuel was at a loss for words. He watched Wilf scramble up the steps and then stood there at the bottom, looking up at the cloudless blue sky above the rooftops.

Eventually, slowly, he climbed up himself.

'I saw Wilf leave without you,' said a voice he recognised immediately, even though they had only spoken a few words to each other.

Samuel turned. Catherine was standing at the open doorway to one of the stables, poking stray strands of hair up under her large woollen hat.

'He did exactly the same to me,' she continued. 'A couple of months ago, when he first brought me here.'

Suddenly everything became clear. He knew now why she had warned him, and the real reason why Wilf had brought him here in the first place.

'I should have worked him out,' Samuel said to himself. Then he laughed.

'Why are you laughing?' Catherine asked.

'The first thing he said to me was that I was the worst thief he had ever met. That's why he wanted me to join Uncle Jack's magpies, isn't it? He didn't want to help me. He didn't want to teach me. He just wanted to have someone around who was a worse thief than he is. That way he always gets fed and has a place to sleep here.'

She smiled. 'Wilf is actually a really bad thief himself. But he's not stupid.'

'Thank you for warning me about him.'

She nodded as if to acknowledge his gratitude. 'Well, I should get going. I don't want to spend another night in there.'

Samuel could smell the stable from where he stood. 'Right. Yes. Me too.'

She started walking. Samuel stood and wondered where he should go. He suspected Wilf would go back to the Royal Exchange or the marketplace.

'You can come with me,' Catherine called back, 'if you want.'

Samuel grinned and caught up with her. 'Where are we going?'

On the way down to the riverbank they talked about Uncle Jack. 'It's quite clever of him, when you think about it,' said Samuel. 'If you have to compete for a place to sleep then it stops you from keeping anything back for yourself, doesn't it?'

'It's a lot cleverer than that,' Catherine said. 'This way, everyone brings in as much as they possibly can, no matter what they have to do to get it. Just wait until winter, when the streets are caked in snow. All the best thieves in that den were the ones who had to steal to survive last winter. I don't know whether I believe some of the things some of them said they did.'

Samuel could imagine, and wouldn't have been surprised if they had been telling the truth.

He and Catherine crossed Thames Street, the busy street of yards and warehouses that ran parallel to the river. The rich smells of tar and spices and oranges and other things the merchants of Thames Street brought back from overseas were quickly suffocated by the stench of the Thames itself as Catherine took Samuel down an alley between warehouses.

The river was brown. A frothy white scum floated on the surface in places, and sticky green algae clung to the wooden wharves and the hulls of moored boats where the filthy waters of the Thames had lapped against them.

Samuel usually kept away from the river as much as possible. To him it smelt of mud and rotting meat and far worse things, thanks to all the little streams and brooks that emptied into the river, but flowed past most of the city's privies before getting there.

'They beat us to it,' Catherine said, gesturing towards the people standing bent double on the mud at the water's edge. 'Let's go down a little further.'

Gulls strolling across the mud took to the air as Samuel and Catherine walked past.

'You're a mudlark,' Samuel realised.

She smiled. 'Well, a better mudlark than a thief, anyway. I always have a look before I steal anything. The other day I found a gold earring.'

'Oh yes, I remember that.'

Samuel followed her out onto the mud, which was thick and cloying where the tide had retreated. He had to drag each foot clear at every step, otherwise he would have lost a clog.

They spent a while digging around, looking for the bounty of the sea, things of value that had been lost overboard on ships and then washed up on the city shore. Most of what they came across was bits of wood and broken pottery.

'What's this?' Catherine muttered to herself as Samuel poked the mud behind her with a stick, hoping to find a chest full of lost gold sovereigns.

She eventually unearthed a large pot, like the one Mr Boyle served their food from. She let out a disappointed groan. 'It's just a dirty old pot. Uncle Jack won't want it.'

Samuel pulled it out of the mud, scooped up some of the fetid river water and swirled it around. The mud lining the pot became looser with each swirl.

'This is a nice pot,' he said. 'It's not broken. We could sell it and give him the money.'

She shook her head and gave him a look that reminded Samuel of the look Thomas used to give him. 'Nobody will buy that.'

'Of course they will. You can always find someone who will buy something, even if you can't find anyone who will buy anything. That's what my father used to say.'

'Was he a mudlark?'

'No, he was a merchant.'

'A rich one?'

'Well, no. But he started off as a pedlar, going from door to door, selling things and buying things. He knew if he bought something somebody didn't want he could find somebody else who did, and he would charge them more than what he paid for it. He was so good at it he even opened his own shop on Eastcheap a few years ago. He can sell anything, my father…' He trailed off, realising he had slipped into the present tense, as if his father was still alive. 'He could sell anything,' Samuel corrected himself.

Catherine didn't say anything for what seemed like a long time. 'My father was the strongest stevedore on St Botolph's Wharf. He could carry me and my brothers all at the same time, and it was like we were as light as pillows. One time on the docks he saved a man from being crushed by a fallen timber beam. He just lifted the beam right off the man…' She trailed off too.

'How long?' she asked quietly after a while.

'Five months next week,' Samuel said. 'My brother Thomas lived longer than my mother and father. He didn't get sick until six weeks ago.'

'My brothers died first. One by one. I reckon they got the sickness from each other.'

'How long?' It was Samuel's turn to ask now.

'Six months. About that. Doesn't feel like it, though. Feels like it was only yesterday.'

Samuel frowned. 'I feel like the opposite. It feels much longer, like it was years ago.'

Again, neither of them spoke for some time. Samuel suspected his and Catherine's thoughts were about the same thing, even if they were not about the same people.

'I'll prove to you that I can sell this pot,' Samuel said finally. 'And if I can't, I'll give you all my dinner tonight!'

Catherine beamed. 'My belly's looking forward to it already.'

But as they headed across London to the Fleet Ditch, and the Rag Fair on its banks where anyone could sell anything, Samuel regretted making that promise. His rumbling stomach reminded him that he had missed breakfast this morning too. He decided to steal some bread when he found a baker's stall. He tried to remember how Wilf had done it.

Fortunately, to Samuel's relief and Catherine's surprise, he sold the pot within minutes. After cleaning all the mud off he gave it a bit of a polish with spit and the sleeve of his tunic. The metal glinted in the sun and caught the eye of a mousy woman wearing a brown linen wimple that covered all but the front of her face. She gave Samuel two small copper coins.

'I suppose I have to give you my dinner now,' said Catherine.

'No. That was never part of the deal.' He held out one of the coins. 'Here.'

'Why are you giving it to me?' She took it.

'That's your half.'

She seemed surprised. 'My half?'

Samuel nodded, and so they continued for the rest of the day.

Employing Wilf's tactic of begging to find a victim, they spent much of the afternoon with their hands in people's pockets. Samuel quickly discovered people were more likely to give alms to a little girl, so Catherine did most of the begging.

At the end of the day they returned to the Three Sisters. They sat in a corner of the courtyard which still caught some sun and emptied their pockets onto the cobbles. They divided the coins equally, but when they reached the last three, Samuel spotted a problem.

'You take it,' he said quickly, putting a finger on the odd coin and pushing it towards her pile.

'No,' she insisted, pushing it back towards his. 'This is the other coin you made from selling the pot. It's yours.'

'You take it or I'll just leave it on the ground.'

She picked it up and then shoved it into the middle of Samuel's pile. He sighed.

The others began to arrive, so Samuel and Catherine filled their pockets again and headed down into the cellar with them. Funnily, the coins didn't feel as much in his pocket as they had looked in the pile, thought Samuel.

In the bowls they looked even less.

When Uncle Jack and Mr Morley appeared, Samuel did not cheer. He hesitated near the back and Catherine gave him a funny look, but she waited with him. Samuel peered over Robert's shoulder. Robert had more than them. When Wilf caught Samuel eyeing up his bowl, he drew it against his belly and covered it with his hand. Wilf had more than them too.

It was of course entirely possible that one of the others had less, and that whoever that was would be the one sleeping elsewhere tonight. But Samuel didn't want to risk it. Just before Catherine passed her bowl to Uncle Jack, Samuel took a copper coin out of his and secretly slipped it into hers. The skills of a good thief could work both ways, he thought.

So he wasn't apprehensive whilst the others waited for Mr Morley's pronouncement. He already had a good idea what it would be.

'Samuel,' Mr Morley said.

Catherine snapped her head round with a look of betrayal on her face. But unlike Wilf's, it was a betrayal Samuel knew she would forgive.

Uncle Jack looked disappointed when he told Samuel, 'Close the hatch behind you.'

Samuel saw the smirk on Robert's face. The ambivalent look Wilf gave him let Samuel know how little the boy cared either way.

Catherine followed Samuel to the hatchway.

'You slept up there last night,' he told her. 'Tonight it's my turn.'

'I should have told Uncle Jack what you did.'

'Go and eat my dinner, will you? I don't want Wilf to have it.'

She glanced back, then gave him a grateful smile. 'Where will you sleep?'

'I know places.' And with that he went up the steps. Catherine was still standing at the bottom, hand raised in farewell, when he slammed the hatch shut.

Samuel ended up in the graveyard of St Michael's, in the long grasses beside the lich gate where he had slept many times before. It wasn't as comfortable as one of Uncle Jack's straw mattresses, but the hard ground didn't keep Samuel awake for long.

It used to make him miserable to sleep here before, surrounded by the weathered grey headstones of the long dead. This time, however, Samuel fell asleep looking forward to waking up tomorrow. This time he had a friend.

Chapter 7

Samuel returned to the courtyard shortly after sunrise the next morning, but when Catherine appeared she didn't emerge from the hatchway with the others. She came up behind him and tapped him on the shoulder. Samuel was confused.

'Did you use the front door?' he asked. 'I thought Uncle Jack didn't like that.'

'No. I ate quickly and left early. I got you a present.'

Smiling, she revealed what was in the hand she had been hiding behind her back. It was a tunic, a little grey from being washed many times, but clean, at least.

'Where did you get it?' Samuel said, shaking it out and holding it up. It was slightly bigger than the one he was wearing. Room to grow into.

'Someone's washing line.' She shrugged coyly. 'They had several tunics on the line, and you only have that one you're wearing. And that's torn. So now you have a new one.'

Samuel quickly unbuttoned his old one and put on the new one. 'Thank you!' He left the old one hanging over the lower half of a stable door.

'I forgot to say thank you last night,' she said.

'This is better than a thank you.'

She smiled again. 'Next time I'll sleep up here.'

'Well, let's just make sure there isn't a next time, then. For either of us.'

Catherine agreed wholeheartedly, but that wasn't the last night Mr Morley called Samuel's name. Samuel wasn't surprised the next time it happened.

Catherine had tried to pick the pocket of a fantastically dressed gentleman in a tall black hat whose loose-fitting rhinegraves had red ribbons hanging from the knees. The man had stopped to peruse flowers on a stall in the marketplace. Samuel picked him out, not realising he wasn't alone. As Catherine's hand went into his pocket, the hand of his lady companion went around Catherine's neck. The lady let out an animal noise. So did Catherine.

Samuel rushed across the cobbles, not knowing what he was actually going to do when he reached them. Coming up behind the lady, his pickpocket's eye spotted the silk purse swinging out from concealment amongst the folds of her black dress. When he grabbed it and gave it a sharp tug he had no intention of stealing it. But his plan worked regardless.

The lady felt the threat against her purse, let out another cry, and more importantly, let go of Catherine. Ducking beneath the trestle table on which the flowers were arranged, Catherine vanished in an instant. And just in time, as armoured city watchmen burst from the thronging crowd, brandishing painful-looking wooden cudgels.

Samuel ran, and the watchmen came after him. They were used to chasing thieves, and they were used to catching them too, but he eventually lost them by running this way then that way in the maze of narrow streets and alleys that surrounded the marketplace. When he ran out of breath he hid in the shadows behind a rickety wooden staircase leading up to a first-floor tenement. Heart thundering, lungs fit to burst, he listened to the heavy footfalls and angry cursing voices charge past.

He spent most of the day in hiding, even after emerging from behind the stairs. It took him a long time to find Catherine. Neither of them had much to give Uncle Jack. Feeling guilty for telling her whose pocket to pick, Samuel gave Catherine the bigger share again.

'Samuel,' Mr Morley duly announced.

'Close the hatch behind you, Sam,' said Uncle Jack.

There could be worse nights to sleep outside, Samuel thought, as Catherine accompanied him to the bottom of the steps. A hot, dry August had recently turned into a hot, dry September.

'At least I'll sleep well tonight,' he said, grinning, 'after all that running.'

'I don't know,' she said, looking up through the hatchway. 'That wind seems to be getting stronger and stronger. You could always sleep in the stables.'

Samuel grunted indignantly. 'Only if it starts snowing in the middle of the night.'

'Goodnight, Sam.'

'Goodnight, Cathy.'

She was right about the wind, Samuel thought, as he emerged from the hatchway. It was almost a gale. Above him the sign for the Three Sisters croaked backwards and forwards. Rustling eddies of dirt and dead leaves swirled across the cobbles. As he turned his face into the wind, grit blew into Samuel's eyes. Rubbing them as he went, he staggered blindly out of courtyard.

When he reached the graveyard at St Michael's he realised he wouldn't be able to sleep there tonight. In the corner where he usually slept the wind was trapped, turning fast circles and sweeping up any loose grass or flowers or grit, just as it had in the courtyard.

As he looked for somewhere else to sleep Samuel passed people rushing home for the night, leaning into the wind and holding their hats tightly on their heads. The wind ripped the cap off another boy's head. The boy chased it down the lane and had to stamp on it to stop it escaping.

Darkness settled over the city before Samuel came across stone steps leading down to the locked cellar of a warehouse on Thames Street. When he reached the bottom of the steps he tucked his legs in and wrapped his arms around himself, resting his head on the crook of an elbow. He closed his eyes against the dust and tried to close his ears against the sound of the wind moaning through the streets. He was glad he was so exhausted. Soon he drifted into a dreamless sleep.

* * *

As the night went on the gale got worse. It tore thatch off roofs and dislodged tiles, which smashed on the cobbles below. White wisps of spindrift blew across the surface of the river and boats rocked in their moorings. Old hornbeams in churchyards stood firm against the wind but their leaves rustled and their branches tapped against stained glass windows.

All across London, doors and shutters rattled in their frames. The wind blew through cracks and gaps and made candle flames dance or blow out. It whistled down chimneys and filled rooms with clouds of soot. People went to bed deciding to clean the mess up tomorrow.

On Pudding Lane, Catherine woke several times in the night, the wind having knocked something over or made a door bang. She thought of Samuel, curled up and cold, and decided that if one of them had to leave the cellar again, next time it would be her.

Further along Pudding Lane stood the bakehouse of Mr Farrinor. Samuel and Catherine had often walked past and slowed down to breathe in the warm, sweet smells of baking bread. It was not something to do when they were hungry. Mr Farrinor baked bread for the Royal Navy. He did not have a shop. They wouldn't have been able to steal from him without breaking in.

Mr Farrinor slept soundly, his nightcap pulled down low over his ears. If he could sleep through his own snuffling snoring he wasn't going to be woken by the wailing wind. In the next bedroom slept his daughter Mary, her big ginger cat nestled at her feet.

When Mr Farrinor had gone to bed that night he'd thought the fire in his smoke-blackened brick oven was dead. After all, the wood had been reduced to grey and white ash, the flames had shrunk to nothing, and no more smoke was disappearing up the chimney.

The first gusts of wind to blow down the chimney unsettled the light, dusty ashes, blowing them out of the dome-shaped oven and into the bakery. They settled atop the bundle of kindling beside the oven, the bags of flour next to the door, and the wooden trestle table in the middle of the room where Mr Farrinor mixed, kneaded and rolled his dough.

Beneath the ashes, at the bottom of the oven, embers still smouldered. Starved of air by the weight of dead ash on top, the last remnants of Mr Farrinor's fire had gone to sleep.

As the wind blew through the night, the ashes dispersed and the embers were uncovered. The next gust stirred them. Breathing new life into them, the wind turned the black embers red, but only for a moment. When this blast of fresh air passed, the embers fell still again and their red glow faded back to black. Had the wind not got any stronger, they might have stayed that way.

Instead the wind got faster and harder. Soon the gusts not only made those tiny smouldering embers flare brightly, but also carried them out of the oven. Those that landed on kindling next to the oven settled quietly on the dry dead wood. Mr Farrinor used it as fuel for the fire because it caught alight quickly. That happened now.

The embers started to smoke and turned into little licks of yellow flame. For some, the wind blew too strongly through the bakery, and blew them out. For others, burning into the sheltered crannies between the shafts of wood, the wind fuelled them, fanning them and making them spread even faster. The wood blackened beneath them, the bark shrivelling. Flames danced, crackling angrily. Puffs of grey smoke climbed up the wall like flickering shadows in the firelight.

Mr Farrinor had piled his kindling precariously. When the pile collapsed, burning wood tumbled out in every direction, and didn't stop until it hit a wall, or the door.

The burgeoning fire burnt through the door of the bakehouse in minutes. Smoke gushed out of the bakehouse's chimney far faster than it had ever done before, but the gale whipped it away. As the flames ate through the bakehouse roof they cast a hot red glare on the lath and plaster rear of Mr Farrinor's house.

Even if Mr Farrinor or his daughter Mary had been awake they wouldn't have heard the determined roar of the fire. That night, like everyone else, they would only have heard the howl of the wind.

As it was, the noise that woke Catherine about twenty minutes later was not wind or fire, but churchbells being rung.

'What's that?' someone said groggily in the darkness of the cellar.

'What time is it?' said someone else.

Catherine sat up wearily and blinked the stickiness out of her eyes. She looked around but saw nothing, not even the first cracks of daylight around the edges of the hatch.

'Don't tread on me!' someone snapped.

'That's my leg!' cried somebody else, perhaps Wilf.

In the darkness Catherine heard the others stumbling about. It felt too early for churches to start ringing their bells. The bells were ringing a lot quicker than usual too, as if someone was pulling on the rope as fast as he could.

A couple of boys had made it to the steps and climbed up. When they opened the hatch an odd red glow shone down on them.

'It's a fire!' Robert hissed.

Excited mutterings spread through the cellar.

'Where is it?'

'How big is it?'

'Can you see it?'

Catherine followed the others up into the courtyard, but they couldn't see where the fire was, nor how big it was. There was a flashing red glare over the rooftops, and a few embers twinkled in the smoke the gale blew this way.

Everyone went out onto Pudding Lane, which was starting to fill with confused people, wrapped up against the wind, wearing coats over nightgowns. Catherine followed them up the street, and then she saw the fire. She froze.

'Someone should tell Uncle Jack,' said Wilf, frozen beside her.

Flames blared from the roof of Mr Farrinor's house, red, orange, yellow and white. As far as Catherine could see the entire back of the house had disappeared behind a wall of fire, which was now encroaching across the roof, swept by the wind. Flames taller than Uncle Jack leapt into the air above it. The black smoke rolling into the sky was lit from within by a flickering orange light.

Only when she got closer, driven by the crowd bustling forward to either help or just stare, did Catherine spot the people in the front windows.

Mr Farrinor leaned out of one casement window, surrounded by a curtain of smoke that billowed out all around him. He looked to be shouting, but Catherine realised he was simply gasping for air.

Catherine saw Mr Farrinor's daughter leaning out of the next window. She had met Mary several times before. She liked petting Mary's cat.

The crowd stopped beneath the windows. Catherine backed off, beneath the jettied upper storey of the house opposite, out of everyone's way. Fire raged through the downstairs rooms but Catherine couldn't look directly at the flames. They were burning so brightly, the furious fire seared at her eyes if she tried to look. Even without the churning smoke that filled the street like fog, the stifling heat alone seemed to make the air almost unbreathable.

As Catherine watched, Mr Farrinor climbed out of his window and perched on the sill. He was pointing and shouting now. 'Save my daughter!'

Men came running from the well in the courtyard. Water hit the flames as the men swung the heavy pails towards the burning building. But it had little effect. The fire retreated for a second, then the wind carried it back again, orange tongues lapping at whatever they could lick, and coating it in flame.

Though men beneath the windows were shouting and gesticulating for Mary to climb out, she just shook her head and shouted back at them. Catherine noticed the bundle of cloth she clutched in her arms.

'Leave it!' the men kept shouting to her over the cacophony of the fire, the wind, the churchbells, her father, and everyone else in the street.

'Please! Someone catch him!' Mary implored.

Catherine saw the cloth bundle move. 'It's her cat!'

Shoving forward, Catherine pushed past Wilf and Robert and the other people gawping as the house burned. She jumped in front of the men who were calling up to Mary, waving her arms. 'It's her cat!' she cried again. 'She wants you to catch her cat first!'

But nobody heard, or none of them listened. One of the men, a burly stevedore, tried to push her out of the way. 'Get out of it, girl!'

Catherine elbowed her way back in front and stretched out her arms. 'Throw him to me!' she called, as loudly as she could.

She didn't know whether Mary had heard her, but suddenly they were looking straight into each other's eyes. Catherine nodded fervently.

Mary bent as far out of the window as she could. Catherine stood on her toes and reached up towards the bundle. The cat squirmed inside the cloth Mary had wrapped him in.

Then she dropped it.

Catherine caught the bundled cat and staggered back, her knees almost buckling under the sudden extra weight. Clutching the creature tightly to her chest, she hurried out of the way. Now her beloved pet was safe, Mary started climbing out of the window.

Away from the burning building, Catherine opened up the flaps of the bundle until the cat's mewling face popped out. His whiskers had been singed, she noticed.

'There there,' she said softly. 'You'll be fine.'

But the terrified animal began to struggle, and she quickly lost her grip on it. The only thanks she got from the sharp-clawed beast was a swift scratch on the arm. Then the cat was gone. Catherine went back to watch the fire. It had now burnt through the ceilings, and flames flashed at the windows where Mary and Mr Farrinor had been standing only minutes before.

Whilst everyone focused on the fire in the Farrinor house, nobody was paying any attention to the embers swirling in the wind above their heads. Nobody saw them settle in the gutters of the house opposite, and there, slowly start to smoke.

Chapter 8

Samuel awoke to a terrible smell of burning. It wasn't the usual caustic smell of burning wood that made his nostrils sting and his eyes water. This was as if everything that smelt bad had been stirred together in a giant pot and left to cook for too long—animal muck, human filth, rotting food, all stewing together in scummy water from the River Thames.

But that wasn't what woke him. Nor was it the wind, which had got even stronger since he fell asleep. It wasn't the distant churchbells either. Thames Street was bustling with people, as if it was morning already. As he climbed the steps to street level, Samuel didn't feel like he had slept that long. Surely there had to be at least another hour or two until dawn. He looked up to the sky to guess the time, and saw only smoke.

For a moment he just stood and stared. He had seen calamitous house fires before. Flames consumed a wooden house in minutes and produced a cloud of rolling black smoke several times bigger than the building on fire. But he had never seen smoke like this before, filling the sky. No matter how quickly the wind carried it away, there always seemed to be more of it.

He cut through the crowds towards Pudding Lane. Most people were going in the other direction. They walked at an urgent pace, as if they were late for something. As he weaved in and out, Samuel picked up on what they were saying in anxious tones. Their words fed into each other's.

'—had to be rescued from the—'

'—full of smoke, couldn't see a—'

'—from house to house, all the way—'

'—almost the whole street—'

'—spread onto the next—'

'—can't put it out—'

An awful lot of them seemed to be carrying travelling bags.

A horrible fear gripped Samuel in the chest as he tried to follow the churning smoke back to its source. He tried to put it out of his head, even as he approached Pudding Lane. But when he reached the bottom of the hill his worst fear came crashing into view.

Houses burned on both sides of Pudding Lane. They burned together, the narrow gap between them bridged by raging red flames. Samuel saw big men, stevedores from the docks, looking like black shadows in front of this wall of fire that blocked the street. They were fighting the fire, quite literally, beating at the hearts of flames twice as tall as they were. Samuel didn't know how they could stand to be that close. Even from the bottom of the hill the fire felt like hot summer sun shining on his face. But it was still night.

Beyond the wall of fire, Samuel could see nothing. The rest of the street was lost behind the shimmer of the heat and the darkness of the roiling smoke.

Samuel started running. He had to find another way around. The Three Sisters was at the top of the hill. It could still be fine, he thought. Catherine might still be there.

On Fish Street Hill, the next street along, two houses were on fire.

Samuel didn't stop running until he reached the top of the hill and the other end of Pudding Lane. He was breathless, but when he gasped for air his chest filled with smoke. He almost threw up.

'Sam!'

Bending over, hands on his knees, he lifted his head. Even though his eyes were watering, his vision blurred, he saw Catherine run up to him.

'Water,' he rasped. 'Water.'

'Give me your arm,' she told him. 'Cover your mouth with your other sleeve.'

He did as she suggested, and let her lead him into the courtyard. His eyes had cleared sufficiently for him to see that the fire had spread in this direction too, but the nearest flames were still three or four buildings away from the Three Sisters.

'Where were you?' Catherine said. 'I went to St Michael's. You said that's where you always slept but you weren't there.'

Samuel needed water before he could speak. He had to wait for a stevedore who had sooty sweat running down his blackened face in glistening streaks. The man filled a pail from the well then Samuel ran the rope down again. He heard the bucket splash into the water a moment before the rope went slack. The bucket had reached the bottom of the well. The well was almost dry. It hadn't rained in so long, Samuel couldn't remember the last time.

'It was too windy in the graveyard,' he explained after cooling his throat with a few mouthfuls. 'I found somewhere to sleep on Thames Street.'

'I was worried about you,' she said.

Samuel drank some more, then the questions started pouring out. 'How did the fire get so big? Where did it start? Why haven't they put it out yet?'

Catherine told him everything she knew, but that wasn't much more than he already knew himself.

Samuel listened and nodded. 'Let me have another drink, then we should help fight the fire.'

'Actually, Uncle Jack wants us to bring his things down and put them on the cart.'

Samuel frowned, and when she pointed, he glanced over his shoulder.

Waiting at the back of the Three Sisters was an old four-wheeled wooden cart. A poorly groomed horse with a shaggy mane and dirty feet grunted and snorted in the smoke but otherwise waited patiently to pull the cart.

A whip across his lap, Mr Morley sat in the driver's seat. In the dim half-light Samuel couldn't see Mr Morley's eyes, but the brim of his hat was pointed in Samuel and Catherine's direction, and it didn't move at all.

'Come on,' Catherine said after Samuel gulped down another couple of mouthfuls.

As they passed the cart on the way to the inn's front door, which was currently propped open, Samuel peeped into the back of it. He had thought Uncle Jack's little magpies always put their pilfered takings into the wooden chest that Mr Morley clung to. It turned out Uncle Jack had several wooden chests, all identical.

This was only the second time Samuel had entered the Three Sisters by the front door. Even though the place felt like home now, he didn't know where they were going when Catherine led him through the empty bar and up the stairs.

At the top of the stairs they bumped into Robert, his ruddy cheeks blown out with effort. His skinny arms snaked around a chest that was really too big and too heavy for him to carry on his own.

'You're not supposed to be here,' he said, stopping in Samuel's way.

Uncle Jack appeared in the doorway at the far end of the landing.

'We need all the help we can muster,' he said to Robert, then to Samuel, 'Good boy, Sam.'

Samuel smirked at Robert. 'Yes. And you look like you need help with that. Here, let me.'

He reached out, pretending he was about to grab the rope handle at one end of the chest. Robert quickly turned away.

'I don't need your help.' He started down the stairs, somewhat clumsily, unable to see where he was going.

Samuel winked at Catherine. She giggled.

'Come and help me in here,' said Uncle Jack.

Two other doors stood open on the landing. In the candlelight of the first room Samuel saw Wilf and one of the other boys helping a woman fold up clothes and lay them in a chest. Samuel had never seen the woman before but she gave him a fierce look.

In the second room he saw a woman who could have been the first woman's twin. They both had fiery red curly hair, they both looked very well-fed and they both wore exuberant scarlet dresses that puffed out over their hips but covered less and less of their bodies the nearer the gowns got to their necks. Samuel wondered if they were the cooks.

'Both of those cases are half empty,' Uncle Jack said, pointing his stick at the black boxes sitting on the bed. 'Empty one into the other then take it down to the cart. Catherine, help the lady in the next room. Do whatever she asks of you.'

Catherine went into the other room.

Uncle Jack certainly didn't sleep on a straw mattress on the floor, Samuel noticed. He couldn't even see the floor. A large woven rug overlapped a smaller sheepskin rug beside the bed. The bed had feather pillows and several blankets, one on top of the other. It reminded Samuel of his bed at home, when he still had a bed, when he still had a home.

When he saw just how much money was in the boxes Samuel couldn't help but think about pocketing some of it. It was what he always thought whenever he saw money now.

'I know how much is in them,' Uncle Jack said, alarming Samuel for a moment. How did Uncle Jack know what he was thinking? It took a thief to know a thief, he supposed.

After a pause, Uncle Jack added, 'So be careful you don't drop any. I'm going to check on how the others are doing in the cellar.'

'Shouldn't we be helping to put the fire out?' Samuel said.

Uncle Jack let out a quiet snort. 'By the time they manage to do that this place will just be cinders in the smoke. In the last hour the fire has spread through five houses, Samuel. It's too close. If we stop now there'll be nothing left to save.'

Samuel would have pointed out that if everybody thought that way and only worried about saving their own things then there would be nobody fighting the fire at all. But Uncle Jack didn't wait to hear it. He turned and limped downstairs, his stick clicking on the bare floorboards as he went.

Samuel tried to lift each of the cases, but the coins inside both made them too heavy. He didn't know how he was supposed to carry all of them in one case. As instructed, he started moving the coins from one to the other anyway, a handful of chinking metal at a time.

After Catherine had helped the woman in the next room carry her chest of clothes downstairs she returned to help Samuel with the money.

'I want to help fight the fire,' Samuel said.

'Uncle Jack says this is the last of it,' Catherine said. 'The fire's only two houses away now. Nothing they're doing seems to be stopping it spreading.'

'They need more people helping, that's why!'

'I know. I want to help too.'

Outside, Wilf and Robert and the other magpies clustered around the cart. The back was now full of chests and boxes and as many wooden barrels from the cellar as Mr Boyle could fit in. The barman sat on top of the barrels, legs over the side.

One of the two women was perched precariously on the edge of the cart, the hem of her dress draped dangerously close to the iron spokes of one of the wheels. Uncle Jack braced against the side of the cart as the other woman used him to climb up onto its other edge.

Samuel glanced around the other magpies and saw their frowning faces, a silent shared wondering where they could sit. There wasn't room for any of them, let alone all of them.

'What about us?' said Robert.

'I have to take all of these things to Mr Morley's house in Whitechapel,' Uncle Jack explained. 'It's not far and it's early, so it shouldn't take us long. Then I'll come back for you.'

He dumped his stick in the back of the cart then climbed up beside Mr Morley. Samuel caught a glimpse of Uncle Jack's wooden leg as it swung past.

'We can't wait here,' Wilf said. 'It'll all be on fire by the time you get back.'

Uncle Jack looked impatient to leave. 'Look, stay together and don't go far. I'll find you.'

Mr Morley didn't wait for anyone else to whine about the situation or the plan. He seized the whip and cracked it hard over the horse's back. Samuel saw the horse straighten its spine and heard it breathing hard as it strained to pull a cart weighed down with five people and all of their belongings.

The magpies watched the cart depart.

'Make sure we haven't left any candles burning!' Mr Boyle called back to them, sounding surprisingly cheerful.

The two women laughed heartily.

When they were out of sight Samuel turned to Catherine. 'Now we can help fight the fire.'

Chapter 9

This was the closest Samuel had got to the fire. His skin prickled with the awesome heat. He felt the surfaces of his eyes drying out the longer he looked at the fire, but when he closed them he could still see the brilliant light of the flames shining through his eyelids.

On both sides of the narrow lane houses were aflame. The fire was inside the buildings, burning outwards. Flames flared from windows and doorways and cracks in the walls. Smoke gushed through the gaps between shutters in gable windows and between tiles in the roofs. The wind swept the flames sideways. Samuel could see how the fire had spread to the houses on Fish Street Hill, and why the men fighting the flames from the ground hadn't stopped it.

'Where are those ladders?' one of the men shouted. 'We need them now!'

'We need more water!' someone else bellowed.

'Give me that pick!' cried another.

'What can we do?' Catherine asked Samuel as they stood back.

'I don't know yet,' he replied, so they continued to just watch.

Everyone moved with purpose. Everyone had a job to do and they knew how to do it. Men struck the cobbles, shattering the smooth flints with the sharp points of their picks. All along the street Samuel saw the cobbles smashed and the earth churned up. Men near the flames wielded shovels, driving them into the ground and pitching clods into the burning houses. The dark soil vanished into the light. If it had an effect, Samuel didn't see what. The flames continued to dance.

'Make way!' came a call. 'Squirt coming through!'

A chorus of 'Squirt! Squirt!' followed.

Stepping out of the way to make a path, the men barged into Samuel and Catherine as though they were invisible. Samuel pulled Catherine into the protection of the nearest doorway.

Two men carried a large brass cylinder between them. It had a nozzle at one end and a plunger at the other and it was as thick as a man's leg. From the look of the men's clammy faces it seemed to be as heavy as a log.

He watched as three men operated the squirt. The two men who had a hard time carrying it had an even harder time holding it up to point the nozzle at the flames. The third man bellowed like a charging bull as he pushed the plunger in with his whole weight behind it.

A thin jet of water shot out of the end of the squirt. It had enough pressure to reach the first floor window and the blazing room behind it. The flames flickered erratically for a moment, but continued to burn. The arc quickly lessened until the squirt was empty.

'Fill it up again!' the man behind the plunger said breathlessly.

'Ladders!' came another distant shout.

'Ladders!' came a nearer one.

'Ladders!' The message reached the front line before the ladders did.

'Here!' the breathless man ordered. Samuel had realised by this point that he was in charge, that everyone was doing what he told them. 'Start a chain!'

'Start a chain! Start a chain!' The message went back along the street.

The men ran the ladders up to the burning roof. As soon as the top rung made contact with the gutter a man climbed each ladder, then another man followed each of them.

An almighty crash drew Samuel's attention further along the street. An immense cloud of flame-rimmed smoke and burning embers mushroomed into the sky above the rooftops. Through the flames he could see the lane was blocked with burning rubble. As the fire consumed them, the houses began to collapse. Wood and masonry tumbled flaming onto the cobbles. Behind the wall of fire Samuel saw the black shells of burning houses shimmering in the heat like ghosts.

Samuel noticed that the men had stopped running back and forth with pails.

'This is where we can help,' he told Catherine.

The men had formed a line, passing full and sloshing pails forward, and empty ones back. But there weren't enough men. Some had to run a short distance to reach the next.

Samuel slipped into one of the gaps in time to take one of the empty pails. He swung it quickly to the next man. Neither the one who gave it to him nor the one who took it off him noticed him. They were too busy concentrating on the pails.

Then a full pail came Samuel's way. He wasn't expecting it to be quite so heavy. He almost dropped it. But he stuck his feet apart and pressed his knees together and managed to swing it. It weighed so much he couldn't bend his arms. After the next man relieved him of the pail, Samuel's arms felt weak and shaky, and the pain in his back didn't disappear.

He didn't have time to think about it, or to watch the pail pass up the chain and then up the ladder too. Another empty pail swung towards him from one direction. Another full one followed very shortly from the other. His heart pounded. He breathed the hot air, the smoke drying his throat. Sweat rolled down his temples.

Looking up he saw Catherine had also joined in the fight against the fire, grabbing handfuls of earth and throwing them into the flames.

Out of nowhere Wilf appeared. He carried another pail, not as part of the chain. He shuffled forward awkwardly, the heavy pail banging against his knees. When he reached the other men he tried to lift the pail and heave the contents into the flames. But he wasn't strong enough either. He could only lift the lip high enough to pour water on the door, which wasn't even on fire.

Though it was a pointless waste of water, Samuel couldn't help but smile.

The smile vanished an instant later. For half that second he didn't believe what he thought he was seeing. His eyes told his brain that the roof of the burning house on the other side of the street was starting to tilt and sag inwards. His brain told his eyes that it was only an illusion caused by the shimmering heat.

Then his ears heard the crunch, louder than the flames. He even felt it in his bones.

'Run!' he cried.

But that just made people look at him, not the burning roof.

Suddenly it collapsed, and in that second the house seemed to burst outwards. Burning timber sprayed in all directions, and then a thick tumbling cloud of smoke and dust enveloped the people in the street.

Samuel stayed ducking on the ground, arms pulled across his head at the last moment. He planned to stay there until his ears stopped ringing and until the smoke cleared and he stopped coughing. But he quickly realised that wasn't going to happen. The smoke was getting thicker.

Covering his mouth with his sleeve again and coughing into his arm, Samuel squinted through the pain and saw the terrible scene. Pudding Lane had been horribly transformed.

Men kicked at burning rubble. Others beat at their burning clothes. The man who had been at the top of one ladder screamed like a baby as people rushed to surround him, hold him down, stop him flapping about on the cobbles in agony. Samuel saw the ripe-red burns on his face. The man who had been at the top of the other ladder lay still until someone started to drag him away from the burning debris by his wrists. For a few seconds Samuel was surprised that didn't wake him. Then he saw how his limp feet bounced over the cobbles. The ladders lay abandoned, just more bits of broken burning wood now.

Then Samuel saw Wilf, and remembered Catherine. Wilf was coughing. His face looked smeared with soot. The whites of his terrified eyes flashed in Sam's direction and Wilf reached a shaky hand toward him, as if asking for help.

'Catherine?' Samuel shouted as he struggled to his feet, but his shout got lost amongst the other, louder shouts of everyone else.

Someone shoved him. Someone else elbowed him. It was chaos on Pudding Lane. Men were pushing to come and help. Others were pushing to get away.

Samuel pulled his way through the crowd angrily. It wasn't until he reached Wilf that he spotted her.

'Catherine!' he shouted again.

She was lying on her side in the shadow of a burning house, her face turned away. Nobody was paying any attention to her. She wasn't moving.

Chapter 10

Samuel's hands shook as he turned Catherine on her back. He did it gently, cushioning the back of her head with one hand.

When he saw the bloody cut to her forehead he froze. She looked asleep. Samuel couldn't breathe, and not just because of the smoke.

Suddenly her face tensed up though her eyes remained closed for a few moments. When she opened them, the tears spilled out, trailing wet paths down her blackened sooty face. She let out a dry, rasping cough.

Samuel almost cried himself.

'Where does it hurt?' he said quickly.

'Everywhere,' she replied groggily, her voice hoarse. 'What...happened?'

'I think you got hit on the head when the house collapsed.' Samuel glanced round to see the remains of the building burning in the street. 'This is all my fault.'

'No, it's not.'

'Yes, it is. I wanted to help.'

'I wanted to help too, Sam.' She winced. 'My arm!'

Samuel looked down at her wrist as she reached toward it, grimacing. He couldn't see any blood and it didn't look broken. 'I think you just twisted it when you fell. Come on, you can put your weight on me. We have to get out of here.'

Lifting her head and seeing how close she lay to the flames, she nodded. 'I think I can stand.'

Samuel stood up and offered her both his hands. They were still shaking, all the fear and excitement still pulsing through his body. He took hold of her uninjured arm.

'Here,' said Wilf, appearing on the other side of her.

She gave him a shocked look.

Samuel was surprised too. He had never seen the serious expression on Wilf's face before. It made him look older.

Between them they got Catherine to her feet. When she stood up straight she didn't need their help, but they both kept a hold as she took her first step.

'I can do it,' she insisted. Her face screwed up again.

'I can manage,' Samuel told Wilf.

Wilf nodded and let go as Catherine took a second step. With Samuel's help she stayed standing.

Something big and heavy crunched behind them, perhaps a large wooden beam breaking in two.

Automatically they all ducked their heads and crossed their arms over the tops of them. Nothing more happened then. But only for now, thought Samuel.

'Let's get out of here,' he said.

'I'm goin' to stay here and help,' said Wilf.

Samuel nodded. 'I'm going to take her to St Clement's church. I think Father Stephen should take a look at where she's bleeding.'

'My head hurts too,' Catherine said, only realising that was what he meant when she touched her forehead and saw the blood on her fingers. She gave Samuel a worried look.

'I'll tell Uncle Jack where you've gone,' said Wilf.

'If he comes back,' said Samuel.

'What d'you mean? He said he was comin' back.'

'I know he did.' As he helped Catherine away from the fire, the smoke and the rubble, Samuel thought that if he was Uncle Jack he wouldn't want to return to this.

It had gone unnoticed under the perpetual twilight of black smoke, but as Samuel and Catherine emerged into the windy open street of Eastcheap they found the sun had risen on another hot morning. The fresh air tasted like clean water. He and Catherine took big gulping breaths.

People got out of their way on Cannon Street. Even if he wasn't bleeding and limping too, Samuel imagined he looked as dirty and smoke-blackened as Catherine did.

He heard people whisper as they passed before hurrying along, sometimes faster than before they had seen him or Catherine.

'Who is this man you're taking me to?' Catherine asked as they turned onto St Clement's Lane.

'Father Stephen,' he told her. 'The rector of St Clement's.'

'Is he a doctor?'

'No, but if you need one he can find one. He can treat some wounds himself. I cut myself badly about a month ago and he helped me.' He held up his hand but the scar had vanished now.

'Did you use to live around here?'

'I used to live on this street.'

Catherine hesitated, then let out a mumbled, 'Oh.'

Samuel hadn't been back here since that day he needed Father Stephen's help, the day the gang of older boys took the stale bread he had been given, the day he learnt to fight.

Despite the bright sun shining between the jettied houses today, despite all those happy childhood memories he had, this winding lane would forever seem dark to him, dark as the night he came back and the door to his home remained shut.

'Which one was it?' Catherine asked after a while, and Samuel could tell she felt uncomfortable asking.

'We'll pass it before we get to the church,' he said.

As they got nearer Samuel slowed down because he didn't want to actually stop.

'It's this one,' he said quietly.

The red paint had finally faded from the door. Rain and wind and sun had left it as Samuel remembered it, just a normal heavy, weathered oak door, with a black iron horizontal bar across the top, another across the bottom, and a black ring-shaped knocker halfway up.

Not that this made a difference to Samuel. In the fleeting moments of darkness when he blinked he still saw the crucifix of blood, as bright and as clear as if it reflected firelight.

'We can stop if you like,' Catherine said.

Samuel shook his head fervently, and they kept going.

With the house behind them, Samuel wondered who lived there now, if anyone lived there. It didn't really matter, he realised. It wasn't his home any more.

St Clement's church looked somehow smaller than Samuel remembered it, but its familiarity made him feel safer, protected even. The church's cloud-grey stone walls had been laid hundreds of years before any of the wooden houses had been built around it. Even the childish graffiti scratched into the stonework round the back had been done by someone who had grown old and died years before Father Stephen was born. The church would still be standing long after Samuel was gone. He hoped so, at least.

Coming round the side of the building, Samuel saw the people heading in.

'I forgot,' he said. 'It's Sunday. He'll be busy.'

He didn't recognise the half-dozen people ahead of them, even though his parents had brought him here since he was a baby.

'Why is that man bringing a box with him to church?' Catherine wondered.

Samuel noticed he wasn't the only one with belongings. One of the women carried a large cloth bundle under each arm. A man in a black satin cloak brought a box with ledgers sticking out of it.

When they got inside they found no service being held, no congregation in the pews. Instead people were milling around the church. Samuel spotted Father Stephen on the other side of the nave, in front of the arched doorway to the steps leading up into the tower and down into the crypt. He was nodding and pointing and trying to both talk and listen to several different people at once.

As he did so, other people emerged from the arched doorway, thanked him, then pushed their hats onto their heads, passing Samuel and Catherine on the way out.

'Is that him?' Catherine asked.

'Yes,' said Samuel. 'We'll have to wait, I think.'

He could understand why she sounded a bit apprehensive. Samuel had known Father Stephen all his life and knew what a kind man he was. But kindness didn't stop Father Stephen looking more like a warrior than a clergyman. A tall man, taller than Uncle Jack, he had bushy grey eyebrows that wisped up at the ends, making him look always angry and fierce. Nobody slept through his sermons, however long they were. He spoke at an unforgiving volume, lifting his long arms, which made his black vestments flap up underneath like giant wings.

They hadn't waited a minute when the verger appeared from the far end of the church, his black gown too long for him and brushing the stone floor of the aisle with a sweeping sound as he came.

Samuel recognised the verger immediately. Elijah was another Plague orphan that Father Stephen had helped. Elijah glanced at Samuel, then looked a second time when he recognised him in return.

'What happened to you?' he said to Catherine. His voice was deeper than Samuel remembered it, and he noticed Elijah was taller too. It felt like years since they had known each other.

'I got hurt,' she said.

'I thought Father Stephen could help,' Samuel said.

Elijah nodded. 'I will tell him you're here.'

More people arrived, all of them carrying belongings. Samuel and Catherine got out of their way.

Father Stephen's eyes settled on Samuel as Elijah spoke into his ear. He lifted his big hands but didn't wait for the crowd to fall quiet. He left Elijah to deal with them and strode over.

'You look like you've been through a battle,' he told Catherine. 'Come with me.'

He put a hand around each of their shoulders as he herded them into the rectory. His powerful grip made Samuel feel safer. Even more than the church did, in fact.

Closing the door to his inner sanctum, Father Stephen shut out much of the hubbub from the church. Samuel had only been in here a few times. It smelt of incense and melted candlewax and leather and old books. Morning sunlight shone brightly through the little window and fell upon the wooden desk and chairs.

'Sit,' Father Stephen told them.

'I didn't know who else to ask for help,' Samuel said, sitting down next to Catherine.

Father Stephen nodded. 'You came to the right person. You're a good boy, Samuel.'

Samuel didn't feel good, and he didn't feel much like a boy any more either. Being here reminded him of a time before thieving, before hunger, before sleeping outside or on the floor of a cellar.

As Father Stephen cleaned Catherine's wounds with a cloth and a bowl of water, which swiftly turned dirty and bloody, he asked what happened, and demanded more detail.

Catherine winced when Father Stephen drew his cloth over her deeper cuts, but they were full of grit and splinters, he explained, and it needed to be done. Afterwards he applied a clear ointment and a white balm, which he got Catherine to smooth into her skin herself.

'Not many turned up for the service this morning,' Father Stephen told them after Samuel finished his story. 'And those who did I sent away. Some wanted to come and pray for God's help to put out the fire. I told them that God had not given them hands, feet, buckets and wells so that they could just sit here and ask for more help.'

Samuel and Catherine both chuckled, and Father Stephen grinned.

'What about those people out there?' Samuel said, glancing towards the door. 'Are they all from Pudding Lane?'

Father Stephen took a deep breath as he sat up straight, smoothing his vestments. 'No, and that's worrying. Most of them are from Cannon Street or Gracechurch Street. They come here and ask if they can leave their things here for safekeeping because they don't think the fire will be put out before it spreads to their homes too.'

'It won't be,' Catherine said quietly. Samuel couldn't disagree.

'Of course I tell them they can,' Father Stephen went on. 'The crypt's almost full now. I don't know whether to let them start filling up the pews too.'

'I think you should,' said Samuel.

Father Stephen smiled at him. 'Well, if you think I should, Samuel, then I shall. Now, what are the pair of you going to do with yourselves?'

They glanced at each other.

Before they could answer Father Stephen said, in a low, serious voice Samuel remembered from some of his sermons, 'I would think you both very foolish to go back to the fire today.'

Catherine let out a little snort. 'Well, you don't have to worry about that, Father.'

'No,' Samuel agreed. 'We did what we could, didn't we?'

'Good,' Father Stephen said, standing up. 'You can of course stay here as long as you need or want to. But I must get back to the people out there.'

As he opened the door and the sounds from the church flooded back in, Samuel stood up. Hunger was starting to plague his thoughts again.

'Do you have any food, Father?'

Chapter 11

With the promise of something to eat from Father Stephen, Samuel and Catherine headed up into the church tower to get out of the way. They hadn't been up there long, watching the fire over the rooftops, when they heard footsteps on the stone steps. Elijah appeared carrying a red and white slipware plate. On it were a couple of loaves of crusty brown bread and a large square of milky-coloured cheese wrapped in wax paper.

Samuel and Catherine sat cross-legged, their backs against the parapet, and feasted on the food. Catherine even picked up all the crumbs that fell in her lap. Samuel ate so quickly he got a heavy feeling in his chest. A loud rumbling belch made him feel much better. Catherine burst out laughing. Samuel joined in.

Their laughs were suddenly drowned out by a sound like thunder. Except it wasn't thunder. Samuel thought he felt the church's stone foundations tremble beneath him.

Both he and Catherine leapt up, Catherine forgetting the rest of her crumbs. Pressing their faces between the battlements they looked toward the thunderous sound, which continued to rumble. It wasn't that far away. In the din were also the sounds of shouts and screams.

'Sam, I'm all turned around,' Catherine said. 'Where's St Margaret's?'

Samuel looked in the direction of Pudding Lane. He knew St Margaret's stood between it and Fish Street Hill. But he couldn't see it either.

'It must be behind the smoke,' he decided, but even as he said it he wasn't convinced.

The pall of churning smoke, darker and taller and wider than ever now, sat over the city like a low, heavy cloud. The wind kept it moving, carrying it away for miles in a continuous and monstrous river of blackness. But it wasn't so thick that it prevented Samuel from seeing the other burning buildings on seven or eight different streets now.

'It's gone,' Catherine said finally.

Both of them took their heads out of the adjacent battlements and looked at each other for a long silent moment.

'But it's made of stone,' Samuel said quietly, almost a whisper.

Catherine said nothing.

All of a sudden Samuel felt nearer to the fire again, no longer observing the flames from a safe distance and from above, like a bird that could easily turn away from the heat and smoke and fly to somewhere else.

'I'm going to tell Father Stephen,' he said.

Catherine came with him.

They found Father Stephen had allowed people to start filling the pews with clothes, food, bedding, even small items of furniture. The nave was starting to look like a marketplace.

The rector received Samuel and Catherine's news with a twitch of his fierce eyebrows but otherwise showed no reaction. He took them aside, away from the people still bringing things into the church, and asked them in a quiet voice to keep reporting to him what they could see from the tower.

So that was how they spent the afternoon, running down the narrow spiral staircase every now and then to tell Father Stephen what was happening. If he was busy or nowhere to be seen Samuel told Elijah instead, and Elijah reported to Father Stephen.

It seemed to get dark early that evening. Because of the smoke, thought Samuel.

Only when the sun finally went down, and the first shadows of night stretched across the city, was the true extent of the fire revealed.

Samuel and Catherine had been watching it spread all day, but it seemed to happen so slowly that they never really got a sense of how far the fire had spread. From above, one burning roof looked pretty much like any other.

But darkness cast the flash and glare of the fire into terrifying relief. Not just one fire, but dozens if not hundreds of individual fires, a long line of them snaking around a countless number of streets. It looked like a giant ripple of flame spreading out in all directions from where it had begun on Pudding Lane. Pudding Lane itself was now invisible in the blackness behind the fire.

'Look at that,' Catherine whispered, her voice inflected with awe.

Samuel glanced at her and then looked up, where she was looking. The mountainous pall of smoke roiling above the city reflected the red and orange light of the roaring fires that caused it.

'It looks like Heaven itself is burning,' Samuel said.

As they stood there looking up, Samuel heard footsteps on the stairs again. Expecting it to be Elijah and hoping he was bringing more food, Samuel turned. But it wasn't Elijah.

'Wilf!'

Wilf reached the tower and slumped heavily against the parapet, breathing hard. He drew a wrist over his blackened forehead. He looked absolutely exhausted.

'The verger told me where you were,' Wilf said finally. 'Uncle Jack sent me to find you two.'

'He came back?' Samuel was surprised.

Wilf nodded wearily. 'Of course he did. He said he would, didn't he?'

'Have you been fighting the fire all afternoon?' Catherine asked.

Wilf nodded again. 'I just need to rest here a moment. Then I'll take you to him.'

The stink of burning, that stinging, piercing smell of smoke, seemed closer now. It clung to Wilf's scorched clothes.

'We've been watching it spread from up here,' Samuel told Wilf. 'It's getting worse.'

'The Three Sisters is gone. You can't get onto Pudding Lane anymore. It's all behind the flames. Everythin' we did was a bloomin' waste of time.'

'You probably slowed it down,' Catherine offered.

Wilf glared at her and slowly shook his head. None of them said anything for a time. Then Wilf took a deep, raspy breath and held his hand out to Samuel. 'Help me up, will you?'

Samuel levered Wilf to his feet.

'Uncle Jack's waitin' in the graveyard at St Benet Gracechurch,' said Wilf.

'Let's get out of here,' said Samuel.

As they headed down the dark staircase, Wilf said, 'He sent me to look for all the others too but I can't find anyone else. Everyone's gone an' run away, I think.'

'We haven't seen them either.'

'Uncle Jack says he's got a plan.'

'What kind of plan?'

'I don't know. He didn't say.'

Samuel stopped before he reached the arched doorway that led into the church, blocked from going any further by the people coming up out of the crypt below. They had the same kind of panicked, anxious looks on their faces as the people in the church earlier, and they seemed to be in just as much of a hurry.

'Sorry!' Samuel said as he slipped into a gap between them. But he didn't know why he was apologising. The man behind him could have let him pass. Instead he scraped Samuel's arm with the corner of the wooden case he was bringing up from the crypt.

The man apparently neither noticed nor cared. He pushed his way through the crowd to get out of the church as quickly as he could.

Samuel went into one of the empty pews. Catherine and Wilf quickly joined him. Only in the pews could they avoid the chaos in the nave, the shoving and shouting, and the impatience of those trying to get into the church whilst others tried to get out.

Samuel realised most of the people arriving came empty-handed. Most of those leaving left fully laden with their belongings.

'Samuel!' Elijah called, squeezing through the crowd to reach them.

'Everyone's leaving,' said Samuel.

'Not everyone.' Elijah looked just as exhausted as Wilf.

Samuel followed Elijah's pointing hand and saw the people huddled quietly in the pews nearest the altar, some of them kneeling, all of them praying.

'Where's Father Stephen?' Samuel asked.

'He went outside a few minutes ago.'

'There he is,' said Catherine.

Samuel watched the crowd part around Father Stephen, as if nobody dared jostle or get in the way of the tall, fierce-looking rector. He headed up the aisle towards the altar. He gave Samuel a quick but grave glance as he passed.

When he reached the front of the church he addressed the small number gathered there as if he was in conversation with them rather than as a preacher. He spoke firmly, but only just loudly enough for Samuel to hear.

'My friends,' he began, 'I believe the time has now come for us to leave the church. I have surveyed the damage the fire has caused so far, and I have plotted its course, and I think in wisdom we must accept that it will reach this place within a couple of hours. Three at the most.'

He went on for only a few moments more, ending with a blessing. Then most of the people got up and hurriedly joined the rest of the crowd trying to leave.

Father Stephen came up to Samuel and the others.

'Elijah, I will need your help until the last person leaves, but the rest of you must go now.' He said it in such an authoritative way that Samuel almost felt safer just because someone seemed to know the right thing to do.

Samuel didn't know what to say. He didn't want to say farewell, as though he would never see Father Stephen again. 'The fire can't burn forever.'

A smile broke out on Father Stephen's face and Samuel felt immediately better.

'Follow the crowds,' Father Stephen told him. 'They're heading for Bishopsgate. Don't stop. Don't wait. Do you understand?'

Samuel nodded.

'Good boy.' Father Stephen turned, his black vestments billowing around him, and Elijah trotted after him towards the vestry.

Samuel turned to Wilf. 'So where did you say we're meeting Uncle Jack?'

Chapter 12

Samuel had never seen Lombard Street so empty, not even last winter when he had kept walking all night to stay warm and then slept during the day.

Wilf led him and Catherine onto Gracechurch Street, where everything was lit a different shade of flickering orange. Stopping only for a moment, Samuel watched the black shadowy shapes of a dozen men in front of the wall of fire that blazed across the bottom of the street. They looked like puppets dancing, but Samuel knew their rhythmic movements were a desperate, lonely struggle to beat the fire back. Meanwhile, beyond them, flames belched into the air above them, twice as high as the houses being consumed in front of them.

'Come on,' Samuel told a transfixed Catherine. He tugged at her sleeve.

Samuel recognised the cart waiting outside the graveyard. It was the one they had helped load up outside the Three Sisters that morning.

As they approached, Mr Morley appeared out of nowhere with a brutal-looking cudgel raised to shoulder height.

Catherine drew breath sharply. Samuel felt an urge to step backwards.

'It's just us,' Wilf said, putting on a snarly voice.

Mr Morley lowered the cudgel and slunk back into the shadows. His unblinking eyes followed Samuel and the others as they passed.

'He's guardin' the cart,' Wilf explained as they went through the lich gate.

'I don't think there's anyone left who needs one,' said Samuel.

'Not here, per'aps.' Wilf shrugged. 'People on Walbrook and Cornhill are leavin' now too.'

In the quiet darkness of the graveyard, sheltered from both wind and firelight by the soldier-like trees standing around the edges, Samuel saw a ghostly glow hovering in the smoky air. As they got nearer he heard the low hiss of mischievous laughter.

Catherine trod on a dry bit of wood, which snapped underfoot. Several people moved hurriedly. 'Who's there?' Uncle Jack's voice growled out of the darkness.

'Wilf. I've brought the others.'

The ghostly light floated up into the air and turned out to be a lantern that had been sitting on top of an old, moss-covered grave. Mr Boyle was now holding it up.

Samuel and Catherine followed Wilf into the clearing, where Uncle Jack stood sucking on a pipe. In his hand he held an axe. Samuel noticed Mr Boyle held one too. It almost looked like they might be planning to fight the fire, except they didn't have a single pail of water between them. Samuel didn't want to imagine what else they might have them for.

'Where are the others?' Uncle Jack said, glaring fiercely from Samuel to Catherine and then turning to face Wilf.

'I couldn't find anyone else,' Wilf replied, his confident snarl vanishing.

'All scarpered, Jack.' Mr Boyle sounded quite amused by the fact.

'We're ready to leave,' Samuel told Uncle Jack.

Mr Boyle sounded even more amused by this. The lantern jiggled as he chuckled.

'We're not leaving,' Uncle Jack said.

'We have to,' said Samuel. 'The fire's coming in this direction and it's coming fast.'

'The fire's coming in every direction, Sam, but it's not coming too fast for us.'

Samuel stared into his eyes until Uncle Jack lowered his head to attend to his pipe and his eyes disappeared into the shadow of his wide hat brim. Samuel wanted to leave, wanted to turn around and go to Bishopsgate as Father Stephen had told him to. But something told him not to turn his back on a man carrying an axe, so he just continued to stare as Uncle Jack took a deep breath.

'This city's going to burn,' he began, sparking a flint into the bowl of his pipe. 'God Himself can't stop these flames now. All of Coldharbour is aflame, or will be by morning. By the end of tomorrow there will be nothing left standing between Thames Street and Cheapside. The ground we're standing on will be covered in ash. The dead beneath our feet will be burnt in their coffins.'

'Stop!' Catherine implored him.

Uncle Jack took in another deep breath, through his nostrils this time.

'All the more reason why we should leave,' Samuel said, shifting his weight to the other leg so that he now stood protectively between Catherine and Uncle Jack.

'No, boy, all the more reason why everyone else should leave,' Uncle Jack went on.

'They have!' said Samuel.

Uncle Jack sucked on his pipe and smoke chuckled out of his mouth. 'I know.'

'What's this plan you told me you had?' asked Wilf.

Uncle Jack leaned against the nearest gravestone, taking the weight off his wooden leg. The gravestone had a stone angel sitting on top. The angel had no head.

'We've been outside the city,' Uncle Jack began again. 'We've seen the people leaving. We've seen the people carrying what few belongings they could grab in the bundles above their heads. We've seen the richest men in all of London sitting atop their carriages, their well-fed children perched between chests of gold and silver and whatever else they could grab in time before they fled.'

Samuel pictured the people going down into, and later coming up from, the crypt at St Clement's.

'You know the people I'm talking about,' Uncle Jack went on, jabbing the mouth-end of his pipe in Samuel and Catherine's direction. 'And you know what kind of houses they live in. Houses like the ones around here.' He made a wide circle in the air with his pipe. 'Big houses. With lots of bedrooms, drawing rooms, pantries. You know how big they are. And you can guess how full of lovely expensive things they are. More than you can fit on the back of a carriage, that's for sure.'

He put the pipe back in his mouth again and didn't say anything more.

In the silence that followed Samuel realised he didn't need Uncle Jack to say anything. He knew where Uncle

Jack was leading with all of this. He knew because Uncle Jack was a thief, and so was he.

'You're going to rob their houses,' he said.

Mr Boyle chuckled again.

Uncle Jack swung his axe playfully, like the pendulum of a clock. 'It's not even really stealing any more, is it?' He sounded a bit disappointed about that. 'They took everything they wanted to save. Everything else, they left behind to burn. They don't want it, and they certainly don't need it. The rich will still be rich tomorrow. But all the things they've left behind are just going to go up in smoke unless we do something about it.'

'Unless we do somethin' about it,' Wilf echoed, his snarly voice returned.

'Are you in, then, Wilf?' Uncle Jack asked loudly.

'Yes I am!'

'Good boy. Good boy.'

'So what about you two?' Uncle Jack said, leering down from his full height and sticking his weathered face right into Samuel's.

Samuel heard Catherine swallow with difficulty behind him. He wished he could turn around, search her face for an unspoken answer. He felt he knew what she was thinking anyway.

'What's in it for us?' Samuel asked Uncle Jack, trying to sound as cocky as Wilf.

Uncle Jack returned to his upright posture and laughed into the sky. 'I like the way you think, Sam. Your brain may be quicker than your fingers, but that's not always a bad thing.'

Samuel almost felt flattered by the old rogue.

'You'll all get an equal share,' Uncle Jack said. 'But this is it. There's no more Three Sisters. No more little magpies. When we get out of the city we go our separate ways. You're on your own, all of you.'

'One cart, one trip,' Samuel said. 'We're not coming back for more.'

'One cart, one trip.'

Samuel paused, wanting to make Uncle Jack believe he was still making a decision, but willing Catherine to make it instead.

Then she did. 'I'm in,' she said quietly.

'Me too,' Samuel said.

Uncle Jack nodded. 'Good.' Then he seemed to lose interest in them. He sucked on his pipe, tapped it against the headstone, then upturned it, spilling the contents onto the ground. 'This must be the only fire in London that keeps going out!' He and Mr Boyle bellowed with laughter, which Wilf tried to join in.

As the laughing went on, Samuel felt Catherine gently prodding him in the back. They sidled slowly out of Uncle Jack's earshot.

'Do you really want to do this?' she whispered.

He didn't answer for a moment. 'Yes.'

'Why? Because you *want* to do it? Or because you don't think he'll let us walk away knowing what he's going to do?'

He paused again. 'A bit of both.'

'I don't trust him.' She started shaking her head.

'I don't trust anyone any more.'

She switched to nodding sagely, then gave him a cheeky scowl. 'Except for me.'

Samuel smiled. 'Yes. It's just you and me, Cathy. Nothing's changed. We mustn't forget that.'

Chapter 13

The dark, narrow alley behind the houses on Gracechurch Street smelt of overused privies, rotting food scraps thrown out of kitchens and left too long in the summer heat, and other revolting things Samuel could only guess at. But at least he couldn't smell smoke and burning any more.

'Watch yourself, boy,' Mr Boyle said sharply as Wilf walked into him in the pitch blackness.

'S-sorry,' said Wilf.

'Next house,' Uncle Jack announced.

He had led the way, counting houses as he went. He held aloft a lantern, but from immediately behind him all Samuel could see were the shapes of his big hat and flapping coat.

Catherine had placed her hand on Samuel's shoulder the first time she tripped. He had put his hand over the top of hers so she wouldn't let go.

'This one,' said Uncle Jack, coming to a stop.

Without any warning he thrust the lantern into Samuel's hand. Leaning against the wall instead of using his stick for balance, he raised his axe over his shoulder and brought it down upon the gate with an almighty crack.

Samuel's whole body tightened as the noise echoed back along the alley. It sounded so loud. Anybody nearby would have heard.

But he wasn't sure what he found more unsettling. That somebody might hear, or that there was nobody left to hear, because everyone was gone. This wasn't the city he knew. It was like a graveyard and these empty houses felt like tombs waiting to be filled.

Uncle Jack struck the gate twice more, and the wood around the latch shattered. The gate swung ajar. Uncle Jack kicked it open the rest of the way with his good leg.

'Try the door, Sam,' he said, slightly out of breath.

Samuel held his breath and licked his lips as he went into the yard first, holding the lantern up as he reached out for the iron ring on the back door. He gave it a hard push, but it didn't budge.

Uncle Jack groaned and asked Mr Boyle for help.

Samuel held the lantern up for them as they took alternate strikes against the door. The rough-hewn oak was a lot stronger than the flimsy gate. The two men struck again and again. The wood began to split but didn't shatter. Another blow and Samuel saw shards fly.

'I don't know why they bothered locking it,' said Catherine over the noise.

Suddenly the whole door visibly shifted. Both men stopped, panting.

'Perhaps they thought there was a chance they might come back and everything would still be standing,' Samuel said.

Uncle Jack left out a breathy chuckle. 'Hope is for fools.'

Mr Boyle sniggered.

'Now, does everybody remember what we're looking for?' Uncle Jack said, leaning on the door and pushing it open.

Inside Samuel could see only blackness, darker than the alley.

'Yes,' he and Wilf said together, Catherine murmuring in agreement moments later.

'Good. If it's not heavy, it's not gold or silver,' Uncle Jack reminded them. 'And if it's not gold or silver, we don't want it, do we?'

He snatched his lantern back from Samuel and opened the metal shutter slowly. Samuel and Wilf lit their candles from the tall yellow flame. Catherine lit hers from Samuel's.

'Right,' Uncle Jack said, finally catching his breath. 'Everyone meet out front once you've found something valuable.' He stepped across the threshold into the dark kitchen and turned right, and the light from his lantern was swallowed by the dead house. Mr Boyle went in next.

As soon as Samuel stepped out of the mossy yard and felt the hard flagstone floor beneath his clogs, all the fear disappeared. It was replaced by heart-pounding excitement. He wondered what riches they would find.

He led Catherine and Wilf out of the kitchen and into the hall.

'Check the bedrooms,' Mr Boyle told the three of them, jerking his head toward the stairs before he went into the drawing room.

Samuel jumped at the sound of something smashing. He saw Wilf pretend he hadn't jumped too. Uncle Jack was in the drawing room already, tipping things over as he rummaged. Samuel stopped worrying there might still be people upstairs at that point. If there had been, they would have heard the thieves ransacking the ground floor.

'Follow me.' Samuel started up the narrow wooden staircase.

The old dry steps creaked underfoot. He took them slowly, not afraid, but not wanting his candle to blow out either. Long waving shadows grew up the walls as Catherine and Wilf came up behind him. The polished panelled wall gleamed faintly with a yellow glow, but in the dark corners the moving shadows looked like scuttling animals fleeing the candlelight.

Two bedrooms led off the landing, both doors open. Samuel could see clothing strewn across the floor in one. It was the first sign he had seen that anyone had left in a hurry, that anyone had left at all, in fact.

'I'm goin' upstairs,' Wilf announced, then he pushed past and headed up the stairs to the next floor. Soon Samuel heard his footsteps across the ceiling.

'I'll look in this one,' Samuel whispered to Catherine. 'You look in there.'

'Why are we whispering?' she whispered, holding the candle up so that Samuel could see the grin on her face.

'You're right,' he said at a normal volume, and grinned back.

He went into the room with the clothes on the floor. Though he remembered what Uncle Jack had said about the kinds of things they were after, he paused and picked up a shirt. It was a lovely white linen shirt with long ruffled cuffs. He wondered if he could get away with taking it, by putting it on perhaps. He shook it out gently with one hand. It billowed out and Samuel saw it was for someone three times his size. He couldn't imagine ever having enough to eat to be that big.

But that made him imagine having enough to eat,

and his tummy burbled, demanding to be fed. Perhaps he could head back down to the kitchen and pinch something from the pantry.

Catherine's clogs clopped briskly across the landing and Samuel turned to see her excited face glowing in the doorway.

'Samuel, quickly, come and see what I've found!' She was whispering again, but it was a hurried, excited whisper this time.

He dropped the shirt and followed her into the other bedroom. This one was much bigger, with the largest bed Samuel had ever seen. It had posts at each corner, a canopy over the top, and finely embroidered curtains around each side. He wanted to lie down on it, just to see if it was as comfy as it looked.

'Look!' Catherine said.

Behind a folding screen that seemed positioned to hide the corner of the room from view, Catherine showed Samuel an ornate wooden table with bowed legs that had been carved to look muscular. Atop the table sat an equally ornate mirror set in a silver frame.

Too heavy to carry, Samuel thought, but then he saw what Catherine was pointing to.

'They were all spilled out like this,' she explained. 'I suspect the lady of the house just grabbed what she could wear before they left.'

Samuel's smile spread so widely and so quickly that he heard his cheeks click. 'This is exactly what Uncle Jack is looking for.'

The silver jewellery box lay on its side, the gold chains and silver brooches and pretty hairpins and jewel-encrusted rings pouring out of the black velvet interior.

'What have you found?' Wilf's voice called from the doorway.

'Come and see for yourself,' Samuel said proudly, sure Wilf wouldn't have found anything better than this.

Sure enough when he appeared around the screen all he carried was what looked like a silver sconce. He had rammed his candle into one of the empty holes. Samuel watched his face when he saw the jewels. He was sure he saw a flicker of jealousy.

Wilf lunged and grabbed one of the rings. 'I'll take this one.' He held it up and admired it.

Samuel snatched it from his fingers. 'We found it. We'll take it.'

Catherine grabbed it from him. '*I* found it. I'll take all of them in the box.'

Suddenly Uncle Jack's voice shouted from the bottom of the stairs, 'Hurry up. We're leaving.'

Wilf turned and stormed off.

Catherine swept her hand across the tabletop, tipping all the jewellery back into the box.

She and Samuel reached the bottom of the stairs in time to see Wilf present his sconce to Uncle Jack. 'It's silver,' he said.

Uncle Jack snorted derisively. 'It's tin.' He pulled the candle out and tossed the battered old sconce to the floor. Samuel swallowed a vindictive laugh.

'What did you two find?' Uncle Jack demanded of him.

Samuel kept quiet about the fact that he hadn't even found a tin sconce, but Uncle Jack didn't seem to care as soon as Catherine opened the lid of the jewellery box. Staring in, eyes sparkling in the candlelight reflected on all the gold and silver, he began to nod and chuckle under his breath.

Shoving in beside Uncle Jack, Mr Boyle began to laugh huskily too. He carried a silver tray with a silver decanter and a few pieces of silver cutlery.

'I'll take that,' Uncle Jack said, snatching the box and snapping the lid shut again.

'What did you find?' Samuel asked.

Tucking the jewellery box under his arm, Uncle Jack said, 'We didn't come here to leave with only a spoon each. We're going to split up. You three will scout out the houses first and let me know whether there is anything worth taking. We'll do twice as many houses that way, or at least take half the time.'

They left through the front door. It looked less suspicious to leave this way, especially when carrying axes instead of keys.

Mr Morley still stood guard over the cart. Uncle Jack showed him what they had got but Samuel didn't think Mr Morley looked impressed at all. He turned back the canvas covering the back of the cart, let them deposit the loot, then flapped it over again.

'Hurry it up,' he said, looking away, into the graveyard. 'Fire's getting closer.'

Samuel looked across the graveyard and saw the trees on the far side were all burning now.

'We'll be quick,' said Uncle Jack.

Back behind the houses they went, further along the alleyway this time.

'Let Wilf into the next one,' Uncle Jack told Mr Boyle. As Wilf and Mr Boyle continued along the alley, Uncle Jack told Samuel and Catherine, 'This one's big. There must be plenty of things left behind. The pair of you scout it out together.'

He shoved his lantern into Samuel's hand again then began striking the door. It didn't take many blows from Uncle Jack's axe before it burst inwards.

Uncle Jack entered the kitchen and grabbed his lantern back so that Samuel and Catherine could light their candles.

'I'll meet you out front shortly,' he said.

Samuel didn't wait until Uncle Jack disappeared into the darkness before leading the way into the silent house.

'Wait for me,' hissed Catherine.

Samuel felt his heart beating fast again. He felt like a buccaneer, like the pirates in the stories his father used to tell him and his brother. He was leading the raiding party, plundering the enemy's fortress for treasure. He felt unstoppable. This was how Uncle Jack must feel all the time.

For a brief moment, as he pushed on into the dining room, Samuel admired the old rogue.

Then Catherine, who was still, spoke in a low, grave voice. 'Samuel, I've got a bad feeling about this. Come and look.'

Slightly annoyed that his hunt for treasure had been interrupted, Samuel rejoined her. 'What?' he said impatiently.

'Look.' She was crouching over a large dirty canvas sack, the kind used to carry coal.

But when she folded the edge back it wasn't coal that glinted in the light from Samuel's candle. It had to be silver. Nobody made such ornate and beautiful tableware out of tin. He lifted the cream jug out.

'What's it doing here?' Catherine said. 'Why didn't they take it with them?'

'Perhaps they didn't have room. I don't know.'

'Or perhaps they haven't finished here yet.'

Samuel sniggered as he put the jug back and stood up. He seized the top of the sack and gave it a noisy shake.

'Don't do that!' she cried.

'Is there anybody there?' Samuel called up the stairs. 'Come quickly! We're stealing all of your precious belongings.'

Beneath his laughter and the loudly clinking sack of silver Samuel didn't hear the footsteps cross the drawing room.

The first he knew of the man was Catherine's panicked cry.

Samuel turned instantly and saw the glint of candlelight shining off the barrel of the flintlock pistol pointed right into his face.

Chapter 14

'Drop it,' said a deep voice that seemed to fill the hall as if it hadn't come from the man's mouth at all.

For a shocked second Samuel was frozen to the floorboards. His hand was made of stone. He couldn't make it obey him.

'Drop it or I'll fire,' the man snarled.

'Sam!' Catherine hissed.

Samuel dropped the sack. The crash and clatter of clashing silverware hitting the floor sent shivers right through to his bones. 'We're going to leave now,' he said, trying to make himself sound unafraid.

The man twitched the end of his gun towards the kitchen. 'Nice an' slow.'

Samuel kept his hands where the man could see them as he took one step at a time, down the hall, into the kitchen. Catherine followed him.

Samuel felt angry at leaving empty-handed. He no longer felt like a pirate, or like Uncle Jack.

'We're sorry,' Catherine said as she passed the man.

'You don't have to apologise to him, Cathy,' Samuel said loudly, so that the man would hear him. 'He doesn't live here either.'

It probably wasn't a good idea to provoke a man with a gun. Samuel hurried Catherine out into the yard and quickly swung the broken door shut behind them. The man did not follow. Of course not, thought Samuel bitterly. He had better things to do.

The wind sucked the flames from Samuel and Catherine's candles and plunged them into darkness as they went out into the alley. The only light Samuel could see was the dim yellow glow from a lantern several houses away.

'Uncle Jack?' he called.

The lantern bobbed quickly in their direction. 'No,' said Mr Boyle.

Samuel heard his voice before his flabby face materialised out of the shadows.

'What's in that house?' Mr Boyle asked.

'Somebody got there before us,' Samuel muttered.

Catherine just nodded.

Mr Boyle held up the lantern and looked at them suspiciously for a moment. Then he said, 'I'll let you into the house at the end. You better find something in that one.'

He took them to the end of the alley, behind the house on the corner of Gracechurch Street and Lombard Street. He had already broken through the gate and started hacking at the door. Another couple of heavy blows and it cracked open.

'And hurry up,' he said. He only waited long enough for Samuel to light his candle, then he stormed huffily off back up the alley.

As Catherine lit her candle from Samuel's, she said, in a whisper, 'Let's be quiet in this one. If there's anyone here, I want to hear them before they hear us.'

Samuel nodded as he looked into the darkness beyond the smashed doorway. 'We don't have to, you know.'

'What do you mean?'

'We could leave now.'

She hesitated, cupping a hand around her candle flame to protect it from the wind. 'Why don't we, then?'

'We could make a run for it. Head for Bishopsgate. We'd never see Uncle Jack again.'

'Let's do it.' She didn't hesitate this time.

But Samuel did. 'We'll need some money.'

'We'll get some later.'

'We could see what they've got first.' Samuel nodded at the house.

After another pause, Catherine let out a sigh. 'All right. But this is the last house.'

'The last house,' Samuel agreed.

With that, they went inside.

All the houses they had broken into were lovely. They looked like they would be bright and airy in summer, but also warm and cosy in winter. Some of them even had glass in the windows instead of shutters. The owners were really that rich.

But this house was by far the nicest of the lot. As Samuel stepped up out of the kitchen and into the main hallway his clogs stopped making a noise. The floor felt soft beneath his feet. Lowering his candle he expected to see a rug, but he'd never seen a rug like this before. It was as long and as wide as the hall, and seemed to fit into all the edges and round all the corners. There wasn't an inch of floor as far as Samuel could see that was not covered by this fantastic rug with its woven chequered pattern.

Lifting his candle as they pushed on towards the staircase, Samuel saw the light gleam off the wooden panels that lined the walls, so polished he thought he might have been able to see his face in the wood. Even the ceiling had been ornately decorated, the wooden beams hidden beneath smooth plaster with circular patterns crafted into it. Samuel had never seen anything like this house before. They even had plants growing indoors. He had no idea how rich these people were, but they were the right ones to rob.

Samuel almost jumped when he entered the parlour and saw the face. Coming in behind, Catherine sniggered.

He cleared his throat, trying to disguise the gasp she had heard. 'Hiccups,' he said.

He suspected she would have had the same reaction, coming in and glimpsing the painting as she turned her candle towards it. It was that realistic. He had never seen such a good painting.

Mounted on the wall, it showed a boy of eight or nine, but the boy was dressed like a little adult. He wore a tight red velvet coat with a frilly white shirt collar bursting from the top. On top of his head sat a giant adult wig of tumbling blond curls. Though the painting was lifesize, the wig made the boy's face look small. Samuel couldn't imagine how much that thing must have weighed. It would have been blisteringly hot to wear in summer. So there were a few disadvantages to being rich, after all.

Catherine let out a little shudder and turned away. 'That's scary,' she said. 'It's like the eyes are staring at you, following you around the room.'

Samuel met the boy's gaze. 'I think he looks sad.'

'I'm not surprised,' she retorted, examining the leather-bound books in a bookcase beside the stone hearth. 'That must have taken days to paint.'

'Perhaps he had an itch.' Samuel chuckled.

Catherine's giggle turned into a gasp, but not a frightened one. A long drawn-out intake of breath full of awe and pleasant surprise. 'Is that what I think it is? It *is* what I think it is!'

'What?'

At the end of the room stood a virginal, its lid open, a few sheaves of music propped up above the keys. Samuel lost interest when his candlelight glinted off a silver decanter inside a wooden cabinet.

'I've always wanted to play one of these,' Catherine said as she trotted over.

Samuel opened the cabinet and took out the decanter. He found a silver porringer too.

He almost dropped the little bowl a moment later when Catherine hit five or six random keys and the discordant noise shattered the silence. He spun round.

'I thought you told me to be quiet,' he said, but not really angrily.

She gave him a mischievous look that he could just about see from the other end of the room. 'Well, I might never get another chance to play one of these.' She began pressing keys one by one, giggling with glee when they sounded tuneful together.

Samuel sighed as he began opening the drawers of the cabinet. They were full of silverware that looked like it had never been used. A grin broke across his face.

'Catherine,' he called over her racket.

As he turned he almost didn't register the face at the parlour door. A boy stood peering in at them.

Samuel froze. He recognised the boy's face immediately. He and the boy locked stares at the same time. The boy had the same sad look in his eyes that he had in the painting.

Chapter 15

In another instant the boy was gone.

'Let's get out of here!' Catherine said, snatching her candle from the top of the virginal but moving so fast the flame blew out.

Samuel heard the little feet scurrying up the stairs.

'Let's go,' he agreed. He cupped his hand around his flame and followed her into the hall.

Catherine glanced up the stairs as they hurried past. The house was dead and silent and dark, but Samuel still felt the urge to escape. He wasn't frightened of the little boy. It was being caught by the boy's parents that terrified him. Catherine was going so fast she half-ran, half-tripped down into the kitchen.

But there Samuel hesitated. 'Wait!' he hissed.

She was already at the back door. 'What? Come on, Sam. He's going to tell his parents.'

'What if he isn't?' Samuel said quickly. 'What if he's alone?'

For a moment he listened to Catherine panting in the shadow of the doorway. That she didn't say anything told Samuel she was thinking it through.

'If they were upstairs, wouldn't they have come down to see who was playing the music?' Samuel asked. 'Why did he come down on his own?'

'What if you're wrong?'

'Listen,' Samuel whispered, and pausing for a few seconds. 'No one's coming.'

'He's hiding,' she murmured.

Samuel nodded. 'From us.'

'They wouldn't have abandoned him, would they? They couldn't, could they?'

'I don't know.' Samuel swallowed. 'But we need to find out. We can't just leave now.'

'Samuel…' she began, but trailed off.

'What were you going to say?'

She sighed. 'Uncle Jack could show up any moment.'

'I know. That's why we've got to be quick.'

No longer afraid of being caught, Samuel walked boldly to the bottom of the stairs. Catherine followed him.

'Hey, boy!' she called up, clearly trying to sound soft, but her voice echoed in the empty hallway.

'He's not going to come down to us,' Samuel said. 'Look at us. We must have terrified him. You're covered in cuts and grazes and I'm all black and sooty and we must both stink of smoke.'

'And we're twice the size of him,' she said.

'I'm going up.'

'Me too.'

After Samuel lit her candle again, they crept up the stairs. Samuel tried to step softly so that his feet didn't make a loud scary noise as they approached the boy.

'We're not going to hurt you,' Samuel said in a normal voice when they reached the first landing.

'I think I heard him go up the next staircase,' said Catherine.

Samuel nodded and kept going.

When he reached the next landing he saw all of the doors were closed except one. He pointed towards it and Catherine nodded.

Stopping in the doorway, Samuel held up his candle, but couldn't see the boy.

'Are you in there?' he said in a quiet, calm and hopefully friendly-sounding voice.

Nobody responded. Nothing moved.

'We're not going to hurt you,' Samuel repeated. 'We want to help you.'

'He's in the wardrobe,' Catherine whispered. The tall wooden closet could have held her and Samuel as well as the little boy. 'Or under the bed.'

'We're sorry we scared you,' Samuel said as they sidled slowly into the room. 'But you can't stay here. The fire's getting closer and closer every minute.'

No sooner were they both inside the room than Samuel heard one of the closed doors creak open, then a flurry of quick, light feet hurtling down the stairs, two or three at a time.

'Wait!' Samuel called, realising what had happened. He chased after the boy, losing the flame from his candle as he ran.

The smart little boy had known they would think he was in the open room so he had hidden behind the closed door nearest the top of the stairs. He might even have opened this door to put them off his track.

Samuel fumbled down the stairs as swiftly as he dared in darkness. He could hear the boy's hurried footfalls a floor below. Samuel was gaining on him.

He knew he had reached the bottom of the stairs when he felt the soft rugs beneath his feet. The little boy had fled into the parlour and wasn't even trying to be quiet now.

'Please don't run!' Samuel said as he followed him in, barely slowing down.

A faint orange light came through the shuttered windows. Samuel knew what that was.

Suddenly he heard a scrape of metal and turned towards the darting shadow. Then something cut through the air with a dull whoosh. Samuel felt it pass within a hair's breadth of his nose. He ducked back and away.

'The next time I swing this sword I will slice your throat open,' the boy warned. His voice shook with fear as he said it.

'All right, all right, I'm backing away,' said Samuel, holding up his hands, even if the boy wouldn't see them.

Samuel didn't remember seeing a rapier in the parlour. Sure enough, when Catherine appeared with her candle and illuminated the room properly, Samuel realised that the boy was brandishing the blackened poker from the hearth, pointing it from Samuel to Catherine and back again and occasionally jabbing it.

Samuel kept his hands up, motioning for Catherine to stay in the doorway. 'You can put it down,' he told the boy. 'I meant what I said. We're not going to hurt you.'

'Then you won't mind if I keep hold of it,' the boy said.

Samuel sighed. 'Fine. If it means you'll stop running and listen, you keep hold of it.'

'What are you doing in my house?'

'Where are your parents?'

'I said, what are you doing in my house?'

Samuel drew breath, trying to think fast.

Catherine was quicker. 'We're going from house to house, making sure everybody's gone and that nobody's left behind.'

Samuel nodded eagerly and pointed towards the glow of the fire that appeared through the cracks in the window shutters. The light from Catherine's candle diminished the distant firelight somewhat. 'The fire's at the end of this street,' he said. 'They can't stop it. All the houses will be burnt down by morning.'

The boy glanced briefly towards the window.

'What's your name?' Catherine asked.

The boy remained silent.

'Where are your parents?' Samuel asked again.

After a moment the boy spoke. 'I don't know.' He said it in a small voice. Even though he still wielded the poker he sounded defenceless.

'They didn't leave you here, did they?' Samuel asked tentatively.

'No!'

'Why are you still here?' said Catherine.

'I had to come back.'

'Why?' asked Samuel.

'He left me.' The boy started to sound a bit upset.

'Who left you?' said Catherine.

'The man.'

'What man?'

'The man with the hackney carriage that my father paid to take me to Brentwood. We have a house there. He was meant to take me.' He sniffed. Samuel couldn't see if he was actually crying. 'We left hours ago. But he only took me as far as the slums outside the city. Then he left me. He turned round and headed back into the city. He laughed when I fell. I tried to catch up with the carriage. But he was going too fast.'

Samuel and Catherine looked at each other. Samuel remembered Mr Boyle's laugh as he and Uncle Jack had left in the cart that morning. Uncle Jack had come back, as he said he would, but not for the reasons he had said.

'You can't stay here,' Samuel said firmly, no longer prepared to be soft with the boy.

'I have to.'

'You can't.'

'When my parents get to Brentwood and find I'm not there they'll come back to get me. This is where they'll look. They're probably already on their way to get me.'

'Where's Brentwood?' Catherine wondered.

'Out in the countryside.'

'How far is it?' asked Samuel.

The boy hesitated. 'I don't know.'

'Listen, your father might be at the end of the street, but he might not be. He might get back before the fire spreads this far, but he might not. So you can't stay here. Nobody's going to fight the flames when they reach this house because there are hundreds of other houses burning down and not enough people left to fight all those fires.'

Samuel saw the look on the boy's face, saw it change. Though he still clutched the poker, the look on the boy's face was now one of acceptance, perhaps even defeat.

Time for a friendly gesture, thought Samuel. He held out his hand. 'My name's Samuel, and this is Catherine.'

'I'm Gideon Fletcher,' the boy said, his thin lips stretching into a nervous smile.

'How old are you?' asked Catherine.

'I'm nine.'

Samuel realised the age gap between him and Gideon was the same as between him and his brother, except now Samuel was the older one.

He took a deep breath. 'You can lower that poker now, but you might want to keep hold of it. Me and Catherine are getting out of this city, before it burns down around us. If you come with us, I will help you to find your parents, I promise. But we have to leave now, before—'

The heavy double thump on the front door made all three of them jump. Gideon dropped his poker.

'Samuel! Are you in there? Catherine!' Uncle Jack's shout was barely dampened by the wooden door.

'Who's that?' Gideon hissed.

Before either of them could answer, Uncle Jack's shouting continued, 'If you're in there, get out here now. We've got big trouble.'

Chapter 16

'Who's that?' Gideon hissed again.

Samuel waved a hand in front of Gideon's face, then pushed a finger to his own lips. He pointed at Catherine's candle. She understood. She blew it out, plunging them into blackness.

'Back door,' Samuel said, no louder than a breath. He hoped Uncle Jack wouldn't hear. Through the door and over the wind, he doubted it.

As they turned, Gideon's boot squeaked on the floor. Samuel froze. 'Quietly!' he breathed slowly.

They tiptoed through the darkness. Samuel felt his way along the walls. Uncle Jack's knocking had stopped. Perhaps he had moved on to the next house, still looking for them, Samuel thought. All he could hear was Gideon's fast, shallow, nervous breathing behind him.

'Who was that man?' Gideon whispered as they reached the kitchen.

Catherine staggered to a stop on the steps and gasped.

Samuel saw the figure coming in past the broken door and for a second couldn't breathe. Then the figure held up an oil lamp. But it wasn't Uncle Jack.

'There you are,' Wilf said, sounding both irritated and slightly relieved. 'Mr Boyle sent me to find you. Uncle Jack's looking for us.'

'Oh, is he?' Samuel said, trying to sound surprised.

Wilf held the lamp up higher. 'Who's that?' he demanded.

Gideon was peering out around Samuel.

'This is Gideon,' Samuel explained. 'He lives here.' As soon as he said it he wondered if he had done the right thing. He couldn't hide Gideon from Wilf, but he didn't need to reveal everything.

Wilf said nothing for a moment, then he said, 'I'm going to tell Uncle Jack.'

He turned quickly and took the light with him out into the alley.

Samuel sighed quietly to himself. 'Come on,' he said, nudging Gideon with his elbow. He didn't yet have a plan, but they couldn't just run now.

Catherine went out after Wilf.

'Is he your friend too?' Gideon asked as they went.

Samuel wanted to tell the truth. 'In a way,' was what he ended up saying.

Though he didn't know what he was going to tell Uncle Jack, he didn't want Wilf to be the one to tell him about Gideon.

Following Wilf, they came out of the alley just as Uncle Jack reached the end house. He saw them out of the corner of his eye and his fist stopped halfway towards a thump on the door. When he turned his head, Samuel saw the fury on his tightly clenched face.

'The cart's gone,' he growled.

'What?' said Wilf.

'Stolen. Some vagabond with a pistol.'

Samuel and Catherine shot each other looks. Both of them were thinking the same thing.

'Forced Mr Morley to the ground then took off with the cart and everything in it.' Uncle Jack made an angry sucking sound then spat on the cobbles.

'The dog!' Wilf cursed.

Uncle Jack finally noticed Gideon. 'Who's this?' he said, his voice soft and suspicious.

Samuel turned to introduce Gideon, but Gideon wasn't even paying attention. He stood facing the other way, staring down the street, mouth open, transfixed. Samuel saw Gideon's eyes flitting up and down, up and down, his gaze following flames leaping into the air from the roof of a house.

'Gideon,' Samuel said, grabbing the boy's arm.

'The whole city's on fire,' Gideon said quietly, looking up at Samuel.

'Not yet,' Uncle Jack said. 'But it will be.'

'They found him in one of the houses,' Wilf said quickly.

Samuel saw the anxious look in Uncle Jack's eyes. It was only there for a second, then the coldness returned to his glare. But the look scared Samuel.

'His parents sent him out of the city before the fire spread too far,' Samuel explained. 'Then he got lost and had to come back. But his parents were gone.'

Gideon nodded, then he repeated for Uncle Jack what he had told Samuel and Catherine about the laughing man in the hackney.

Samuel kept watching Uncle Jack's face. Uncle Jack didn't take his eyes off Gideon, didn't even blink. He nodded and frowned in all the right places, as though he was outraged by Gideon's misfortune.

'Well, Sam's right,' Uncle Jack said after Gideon finished. 'You can't stay here.'

But it was what he said next that shocked Samuel.

'You will have to come with us.'

'Are you going to Brentwood?' Gideon asked.

'I don't know where that is,' Uncle Jack said. 'But I intend to find out.'

'Are we leaving now?'

For the first time in over a minute Uncle Jack took his eyes off Gideon and looked at the rest of them too. 'Mr Boyle has gone to look for another cart. Wilf, I want you to go and help him. We saved a lot from our house and I'd rather not leave without it.' Uncle Jack's lips curled into a smile. 'Mr Morley is guarding our things in the churchyard at St Edmund's. We will take Gideon there and wait.'

Gideon beamed. 'I think my father will give you a reward for helping me.'

'Will he?' said Uncle Jack, sounding pleasantly surprised. He cocked his head and they all started walking.

Gideon caught up with Uncle Jack and walked beside him. 'Oh yes. He's very rich, you know.'

'Is he?' Uncle Jack sounded even more surprised about that.

Wilf walked on Uncle Jack's other side. Samuel paused, letting them get some way ahead. When Catherine started to follow, Samuel held a hand out to stop her.

'What?' she said.

Samuel let the others get a little more distance, then when he couldn't make out the words they were saying, he started after them.

'We could still run,' he said flatly. 'Right now.'

'We're not going to, though, are we?'

He looked at her. 'You could. You should. I'll come up with a good story.'

She sighed. 'I'm not going to leave now for the same reason you're not going to.'

'I wish I could say I wish we'd run when we had the chance, that we'd never gone into that house—'

Catherine finished his sentence for him: 'But Gideon would have died if we hadn't found him.'

'That's why I couldn't say it.'

Uncle Jack and the others turned the corner onto Lombard Street. Samuel found himself quickening his pace, not wanting to let Gideon out of his sight.

'He's only a little boy,' Samuel muttered.

'You remember what we said about Uncle Jack, don't you?' Catherine said quietly.

Samuel nodded. 'I don't trust him. I don't think he's helping Gideon out of the goodness of his heart. I don't know what he's doing yet—'

Again, Catherine finished his sentence for him: 'But it won't be good.'

Chapter 17

Downwind of the fire, the churchyard of St Edmund's sat in a flowing tide of smoke. Uncle Jack led Samuel and the others quickly through the dense cloud. His yellow lantern light didn't penetrate far through the ghostly gloom. Gideon soon started to cough.

Another flickering orb of light appeared ahead of them and then the church itself loomed out of the darkness.

'Jack?' Mr Morley's voice called out.

'Aye,' Uncle Jack called back.

The church's tall stained glass windows looked black in the night. No light came from inside. Samuel spied the ugly gargoyles sitting atop the eaves, glaring down at the new arrivals.

Mr Morley leant against the wall. In the doorway beside him stood a stack of wooden boxes, all different sizes, covered with a blanket that flapped in the wind. They had got a lot of loot, thought Samuel, even after losing everything that had been in the cart.

'Now you know where we are you can find your way back,' Uncle Jack said to Wilf.

'Which way did Mr Boyle go?' asked Wilf.

Mr Morley pointed his axe into the darkness and without another word Wilf vanished in that direction.

'And hurry,' Uncle Jack shouted after him, 'or we'll leave without you.'

Mr Morley laughed hoarsely. He had a trickle of blood running from a dark cut that matted the hair around his left temple. Samuel thought he looked like he was afflicted by nagging pain on good days, but now his nostrils flared and his narrow eyes bulged with rage.

Gideon coughed again.

'The three of you go and wait inside,' Uncle Jack said. 'Get Gideon out of this smoke.'

Samuel and Catherine obediently opened the church door. The rusty iron hinges creaked. Gideon hesitated.

'What's wrong?' Samuel asked.

Gideon glanced up at Uncle Jack. 'It's dark in there.'

Uncle Jack smiled down at him, then thrust his lantern towards Samuel. 'Light some candles.'

As Samuel pulled the creaking door shut behind them he heard Mr Morley ask, in a low voice, 'So who's the new stray, Jack?'

The heavy oak door muffled Uncle Jack's answer.

Samuel sighed. The others waited for him. 'Let's light a few candles, then.'

The nave stood empty and dark and silent except for the sound of the gale outside. Samuel could imagine voices raised in song and a rector like Father Stephen preaching from the lectern. But that just made the place seem even more lifeless without these sounds, without the people.

Samuel's clogs clacked on the stone floor and the noise echoed sharply. He approached the tall candles at the end of the aisle and carefully opened the shutter on Uncle Jack's lantern to light them. Then Catherine picked up one of the candles and went down the aisle, lighting others.

Gideon followed them wherever they went.

'Why don't you go and sit down?' Samuel suggested. Gideon took it as an order and slipped into the nearest pew.

Samuel and Catherine reached the altar. For a moment it felt wrong to light these sacred candles, the kind Samuel had watched lit every week as a child at St Clement's. But at least the shadows of the church seemed less oppressive after he had done it.

He was also glad to get Catherine away from Gideon.

'I've got a plan,' he whispered.

She grinned. 'I thought you might.'

'We tell Uncle Jack that Gideon has the Plague. We can tell him we saw the purple lumps under his arms and that's why the man abandoned him. Uncle Jack won't want to go anywhere near him then.'

Catherine didn't say anything for a long time, just looked at Samuel. 'Is that it?'

'I know we'll have to get Gideon to play along, but he's already been coughing.'

'Because of the smoke!'

'Well, we'll have to get him to start sneezing, then.'

'And what if Uncle Jack wants to look under his arms? He doesn't have any signs of Plague.'

Samuel shook his head. 'Uncle Jack won't want to get that close if he thinks Gideon has the Plague.'

She sighed. 'It's not going to work, Sam. Uncle Jack knows what someone who has Plague looks like. Gideon doesn't look sick at all.'

Samuel glanced back at him. Gideon sat up in the pew and smiled brightly. Samuel felt something sink inside. He knew Catherine was right.

'Perhaps Father Stephen is still at St Clement's,' she said. 'Perhaps he can help.'

'And what if he's gone? What if St Clement's is, too?'

She didn't have an answer for that.

'How long do we have to wait here?' Gideon asked. He was standing in the aisle now.

'As long as Uncle Jack wants,' Samuel said curtly.

He had to turn Gideon against Uncle Jack somehow. The boy looked up to the old thief as if he was a hero, rescuing him, protecting him. But Samuel would then have to come up with a good explanation for why he and Catherine had been in Gideon's home too.

Gideon joined them at the front of the church. 'Your uncle is a good man.'

'He's not our uncle,' said Catherine.

Gideon looked a bit confused. 'You called him your uncle. So did your other brother.'

'What brother?'

'The other boy. The one that ran off.'

Samuel laughed. 'Wilf! Who'd want him for a big brother?'

'Wilf's not my brother,' Catherine said. 'Neither is Sam. And Jack's not my uncle. None of us are from the same family.'

Gideon looked even more confused. 'So how do you two know each other?'

Samuel and Catherine swapped glances. 'We're friends.'

'Well, why are you running around at night? Where are your mothers and fathers?'

Samuel could see Catherine was no longer amused by Gideon's innocence and confusion. 'I'm going to go and watch the fire from the tower,' she announced.

'Can I come?' Gideon asked excitedly.

Samuel reached out and held his arm. 'No, stay here.'

They watched her hurry along the aisle and up the stone steps into the tower. After she had gone, Samuel motioned for Gideon to retake his seat in the pews. Samuel went into the one in front, knelt on the hard wooden bench and leant over the back.

'Were you living in the city a year ago?' he asked.

'No. We went and lived in Brentwood. That's where we're going now, isn't it?'

Samuel nodded. 'Did your mother and father tell you why you had to move out of the city?'

Gideon shook his head. 'It's nice in the country.'

'What do you know about the Plague?'

'I heard it makes your fingers fall off.'

Samuel sat down properly and took a deep breath. He wished he was in the tower with Catherine. 'Do you know what an orphan is, Gideon?'

***

Up in the tower, Catherine stared over the parapet toward the fire. All she saw behind a blur of tears was the almighty orange light. She tried to swallow her sobs. Taking a deep steadying breath she closed her eyes and lifted her face, letting the wind dry the wet streaks from her cheeks.

When she wiped her eyes on her bare wrist she could see the flames again. Like a living forest shaken by the wind, the towering flames spread in an arc as far as she could see. All the houses disappeared in the darkness, the black cauldron of smoke broiling in the air beyond.

She took another deep breath and started back down the spiral staircase, feeling her way down the cold stone wall.

As she passed the narrow slit of a window above the church entrance she heard Mr Morley's voice. He seemed to be in an argument with Uncle Jack. Catherine stopped on the stairs and listened, her heart beating fast.

'One of us will go and collect the money,' Uncle Jack was saying. 'The rest of us will stay with the boy. Once the gold is ours, we let the boy go. Simple.'

Mr Morley grumbled something she couldn't make out, then continued, 'It's never that simple, Jack.'

Uncle Jack tried to interrupt. Mr Morley went on over the top of him, saying loudly, 'They'll hunt us down like animals.'

Catherine wanted to run down the steps but she couldn't move.

'I reckon his parents are smart people,' Uncle Jack went on. 'Unless they come up with the gold, as far as they or anyone else will be able to prove, their precious little prince went up in smoke with the rest of the city.'

It took Catherine as long as Mr Morley to realise what Uncle Jack meant. She lifted a trembling hand to her mouth.

Mr Morley started to laugh. After a moment, Uncle Jack joined in.

Catherine regained control of her legs. Slowly, carefully, anxious not to make a sound, she picked her way down the steps.

Chapter 18

Samuel thought he saw Gideon's eyes glisten with tears in the candlelight. The little boy had listened in silence, not moving at all, his hands clasped in his lap.

'And much the same happened to my family too,' Samuel continued. 'I learnt from Father Stephen that my mother caught it first. He didn't know where from. My father wouldn't leave her. So he caught it from her. I don't know how my brother got sick, and why I didn't, because we were together all the time. As soon as he fell ill he made them take him away so I wouldn't get sick too. After that I never saw him again. Father Stephen said he wrote me a letter but that they were worried it had Plague on it so they burnt it. He never got to read it, so he couldn't tell me what was in it. Now I'll never know. I don't suppose it matters in the end, really.'

'Yes it does,' Gideon said, his voice sounding small but still sure of himself. 'He probably said something like he didn't want you to be sad.'

Samuel smiled. 'Knowing my brother, it was probably a warning to keep my hands off his clogs!'

Gideon grinned.

Out of the corner of his eye Samuel saw Catherine appear at the bottom of the steps. Gideon saw him looking in that direction and turned.

'I should say sorry for making her sad,' he said quietly.

When Samuel saw the distracted look on her face as she came silently down the aisle he reached out and suggested the boy wait.

Gideon stood up as she approached, ignoring Samuel. 'I didn't mean to make you sad.'

She gave him an almost confused glance, as if she had no idea what he was talking about. Samuel could see the dried tearstains in the dirt and soot on her face, but she didn't look upset now. She looked worried, very worried.

Ignoring Gideon, she said, 'Sam, can I have a word with you?'

'What's wrong?' Samuel asked.

'Over there.' She cocked her head toward the pulpit.

'Is it a secret?' Gideon asked.

'No. Nothing like that.'

'I can keep a secret.'

'Wait here,' Samuel told him.

Catherine went ahead, stopping only when she reached the altar. She stood staring into the candle flame until

167

Samuel caught up with her, then she turned and checked Gideon was still sitting where they had left him.

'What is it?' Samuel asked.

'Keep your voice down,' she murmured.

Samuel glanced back at Gideon. 'It's about him, isn't it?'

She gave a little nod, as if she didn't want Gideon to see. 'I was up in the tower. When I came down I overheard Uncle Jack and Mr Morley talking. About Gideon.' She hesitated. 'I heard Uncle Jack's plan.'

'What plan?'

'He wants gold, lots of gold, for taking Gideon home.'

Samuel nodded. 'Well, Gideon did say his father would probably give us a reward.'

'Sam, it's not a reward they're after,' she said, her whisper turning into a hiss. 'It's a ransom.'

'A ransom?'

'Yes. A reward is what they'd give Uncle Jack for bringing Gideon home after he's done it. It's not a reward if Uncle Jack won't take him home until Gideon's father gives him the money.'

Samuel stared at her for a moment. 'He'd do that?'

She nodded slowly, then swallowed hard. 'It gets worse.'

Samuel glanced round. Gideon was in the pew, straining to hear what they were saying. The look of annoyance on his face suggested he couldn't.

'I think they might kill him,' Catherine muttered.

'They wouldn't!' Samuel said, a bit too loudly. Gideon perked up. Samuel lowered his voice. 'Uncle Jack is a thief, a cheat and he probably was a smuggler once upon a time too, but he's not a murderer. I doubt even Mr Morley could kill anyone, especially not a little boy.'

'How do you know that, Sam? We don't really know anything about any of them, do we?'

'Uncle Jack was in the Royal Navy. He lost his leg in a sea battle.'

'So Wilf says. And who told him? Everything we know about Uncle Jack we heard from someone else. He hides behind the story. It makes him seem mysterious and scary. We don't even know his last name!'

Samuel stared at his feet. 'I'm going to talk to him.'

He started down the aisle at a marching pace. Perhaps Catherine thought he meant Gideon, because she didn't call out for him to wait until he passed the pew where Gideon sat. It wasn't until he reached the door and had his hand on the iron handle to pull it open that Samuel felt the fear in his heart.

He opened the door anyway.

Uncle Jack stiffened and Mr Morley hunched up, arms folding like entangling snakes. Samuel could imagine the two men conspiring as Catherine had described it for him.

'What do you want, Samuel?' Uncle Jack said.

'I just wanted to see if Mr Boyle had found a cart yet.' Samuel was disappointed his voice sounded so meek.

'No. Go back inside and wait with the others. I'll let you know when it's time to leave.'

'What if they can't find a cart?'

'Then we're leaving anyway.' Uncle Jack gestured towards the orange glow behind the buildings. It was not the sunrise. 'The fire's getting too close.'

That was all Samuel needed to hear. If Uncle Jack was willing to leave all this loot behind then it was because he had found a better way to make money.

Samuel nodded and turned back to the door. What Uncle Jack said then made Samuel realise exactly what kind of man he was.

'How's Gideon?'

'He's fine,' Samuel said flatly, then he went inside and shut the door.

As he approached the other two he saw the expression on Catherine's face, a mix of anger, sadness and fear. The puzzled look on Gideon's face told Samuel she hadn't told him.

When he reached them he didn't stop walking.

'We need to find the back way out of this place,' he said, as he continued up the aisle.

Chapter 19

When Catherine told Gideon why they had to leave, he stopped following them.

'You were stealing from my house,' he said, standing in the middle of the aisle.

Samuel had reached the door to the vestry but he stopped and turned.

'We had to,' Catherine lied. 'He was forcing us to.'

Samuel nodded. The absolute truth would not help them convince Gideon now. 'Remember when Jack knocked on the door? Instead of answering we crept through the house and went out of the back door. We were going to run from Jack then, and take you with us. The only reason we couldn't is because we bumped into Wilf. Now, we've got to hurry. Wilf and Boyle could be back with a cart any minute now.'

'Come on.' Catherine held her hand out to Gideon.

Samuel opened the vestry door. The light from the nave barely penetrated the darkness, but firelight glowed faintly through a little stained-glass window. That green glow was enough for Samuel to see the back door.

'I don't know if I can trust you,' Gideon protested. 'How do I know you won't just try and ransom me back to my family too?'

Samuel turned back. 'Don't trust us, then,' he said impatiently. 'And don't come with us. We're leaving now and I suggest you do too. Whether you come with us is up to you. Come on, Cathy.'

He hoped that would be enough. Taking up one of the candles, he went into the vestry.

'Come with us,' Catherine said to Gideon.

Samuel didn't hear Gideon respond, but when Catherine joined Samuel in the clergyman's office Gideon was with her, his face set, his expression resolute.

'Here, hold this,' Samuel told Catherine, giving her the candle.

He hoped the door was just stiff. Turning the iron ring one way, he pulled. Turning the iron ring the other way, he pulled. Then he turned it both ways again, pushing both times. The door didn't even rattle in the frame.

'Locked,' he said under his breath. 'There must be a key around here somewhere.' He ran his fingers over the keyhole. 'It'll be a big one.' As he looked around the room he saw Gideon peering around the vestry door, watching in case Uncle Jack came into the church.

'Bring that over here,' Samuel told Catherine, beckoning her over to the cluttered draw-table.

She held the candle above the mess of loose sheaves of paper and unsteady piles of leather-bound books as Samuel sifted through. At first he lifted up individual sheaves, as if the key had been slipped underneath. But, finding nothing, he quickly began sweeping piles of paper off the desk. They fluttered in the air and settled on the flagstone floor like autumn leaves.

'Where is it?' he said to himself, opening books as if it would be sitting between the covers and the front pages, then knocking them aside when it wasn't there. He shook a few, in case it was hidden between later pages.

The key was nowhere to be found.

'Sam, we have to face the fact that perhaps the Father took it with him,' Catherine said.

Samuel said nothing in response, staring at the little window above the table. He looked from there to Gideon, then the wooden chair in front of the table.

'He can fit through there,' Samuel said, then he picked up the chair.

'What are you doing?' cried Catherine. 'Uncle Jack will hear the glass break.'

Samuel was glad to lower it again for a second. The chair was heavier than it looked. 'It doesn't matter. Gideon will be gone before they get here.'

'And what about us? I don't know if I can fit through that window but you won't be able to. He'll know what we did and he'll know why. What will he do with us then?'

'I don't want to go on my own,' Gideon said. 'I don't know the way.'

'We're all going,' Catherine said firmly.

Samuel nodded and let the chair come to a gentle rest on the floor. 'But how?' he said, mostly to himself.

None of them said anything for a moment.

'We've got to get them away from the front of the church,' he said.

'A distraction,' said Catherine.

'Smash the window,' Gideon suggested. 'That will make them come running, like you said.'

'And leave whoever smashes it cornered in here with them.'

Samuel shook his head. 'What we need is for one person to distract them whilst the other two sneak out behind them.'

'But they need to be distracted by something else, not one of us, or whoever it is will still be cornered.'

'Unless…' Samuel trailed off. 'I've got it.'

'What is it?' Catherine and Gideon said together.

Samuel rushed past them, back out into the nave. He went so fast his candle blew out, but he just dumped it on the altar as he passed. 'Come with me,' he called back. 'I need to see if we can get into the crypt.'

Sure enough he found that the stone steps that led up into the church tower also disappeared into the darkness of the crypt below. Even better, the steps were right beside the way out.

'What's the plan?' Gideon asked in a loud whisper.

Samuel went and blew out the candles at the back of the church, plunging the last few pews into shadow. Catherine and Gideon followed him as he slipped into the last of those dark pews.

'Here's what you're going to do,' he said. 'You're both going to hide here, crouch down where they won't see you when they come in. Then I'm going to go out there and tell them Gideon has fallen in the crypt and I think he's broken his leg.'

'Why me?' he asked.

'Because you're worth a lot more to them than we are,' Samuel replied.

Catherine nodded grimly.

'I'll make sure both of them come in,' Samuel went on. 'Jack will want to make sure you are not going to bleed to death or anything, but with his stick he won't be able to carry you up, so he'll need Morley to do that. As soon as they go down, both of you must run.'

'What about you?' said Catherine.

175

'I'll start following them down into the crypt. I'll have to judge the right moment to turn and run, because as soon as they get down there and see Gideon's not there they'll work out what we've done.'

'But you'll only be just ahead of them.'

'Morley is old and Jack has his stick. I can outrun both of them.'

Again, none of them said anything for a moment.

'It's a good plan,' Gideon decided finally.

'Then let's do it.' Samuel got up and vaulted over the back of the pew. 'Get down and be quiet.'

'Sam, wait,' said Catherine.

'What for?'

She licked her lips and swallowed. 'I think I should be the one to distract them.'

'No,' he said immediately, then, 'Why?'

'Because I can run faster than you, and I can run faster than them too,' she began, then after a pause added, 'And if Gideon needs protection then he needs you to be with him.'

They stared at each other.

'Let's go,' Gideon said urgently.

'We'll wait for you outside,' Samuel told Catherine. He knew her argument made sense.

She shook her head. 'No. Don't wait. Run. I'll catch up with you. Let's meet at Bishopsgate.'

'No, that's too close. It's the shortest route out of the city. That's the way they'll think we'll go.'

'Ludgate, then. It's the furthest. They'll never think we'd go that way.'

'St Paul's,' Samuel said with a smile. 'It's on the way. Let's meet there.'

She smiled back. 'On the steps at the front.'

'Yes! You won't be able to miss us.'

'All right. You two hide.'

She and Samuel switched places.

'Get down,' Samuel told Gideon as he lowered himself onto the cold stone floor.

Gideon squatted into a small shape in front of Samuel. As he lay there, Samuel felt the dust tickling the inside of his nose, making his whole face twitch with the threat of a sneeze.

All of a sudden this seemed like a terrible idea. Even if he managed not to sneeze and Gideon managed not to sneeze and neither of them made any other noise either, he still felt obvious and visible and exposed.

But it was too late to change the plan now.

'Help!' Catherine cried as she yanked the creaking door open. 'Help! Quickly!'

Samuel held his breath, but he wasn't sure he could have breathed even if he had wanted to. Gideon was panting in terror. Samuel was certain Uncle Jack would hear.

Catherine only took a moment to gabble her story on the other side of the door. The door banged open. Feet thundered in at a rush. Samuel could make out more than one pair, and the rapid scrape and click of Uncle Jack's stick.

'Down here!' Catherine said.

Samuel waited, heart pounding, arm and leg muscles tensed, ready to leap up.

Then he heard feet on steps, clattering downwards.

'Go!' he hissed.

He was ready to grab the back of Gideon's tunic, pull him to his feet if he had to, but Gideon sprang up even more quickly than Samuel.

Out of the pew, down the aisle they scurried. Samuel charged so fast he almost collided with the door.

In another second he had it open, and he and Gideon were out into the night and the smoke.

There was nobody else there. They had done it.

'This way!' Samuel said, and away they ran.

Out of the corner of his eye Samuel saw a figure in a dark alley as they ran past, but he didn't give the person a second glance, or a second thought.

Chapter 20

Samuel and Gideon ran and did not stop. They passed a trail of abandoned furniture, including wooden chairs lying on their sides, a washboard that had been left propped against a wall and a rolled-up rug which had begun to unfurl over the cobbles.

Samuel could have run faster, but he felt a need to keep Gideon in front of him, where the boy wouldn't go out of his sight, where he wouldn't be seen by anyone coming up behind. As Gideon panted like a dray horse, elbows digging backwards with the effort, Samuel dared to glance behind them. Nobody was behind them. But he didn't feel any sort of relief. The dark abandoned street was empty in a way Samuel had never seen it, not even in the depths of wintry nights, but that didn't make him feel safer. There was nobody to chase them, but there was nobody to help them either. They were alone, in a way Samuel hadn't felt alone since immediately after he lost his brother.

Suddenly, as they came to the end of Lombard Street, the street ahead became full of light and noise and people again. For a moment Samuel saw the crowd as a place to hide.

Then they got closer, and the noise of the crowd grew louder than the wind. It was an undeniably angry noise, dozens of shouting voices, and as he and Gideon went from Lombard Street to Poultry, Samuel saw the crowd change from a single group to a pushing, shoving swarm of furious individuals.

'What's going on?' Gideon said, slowing to little more than a brisk walk.

'I don't know,' said Samuel. 'But that's the way we have to go.'

They were near enough now for him to see two carts blocking the junction with Walbrook and Threadneedle Street. Obviously neither had stopped, even though they had been trying to cross each other's paths. One lay on its side, the other's horse lying beside it, not moving.

At the edge of the crowd Samuel found people with bags and crates and barrows unable to get past the blockage. The street was too narrow. Curses filled the air. Everyone was shouting at everyone else. Nobody was listening.

A scream cut through the din.

Gideon grabbed Samuel's arm. 'Let's go.'

Samuel saw a cudgel raised above the heads of other people, saw it come down. The sudden fury of the mob seemed infectious. Even those at the back pushed forward.

'It's all falling apart,' Samuel said, seizing Gideon by the shoulders and guiding him out of the swelling crowd. 'Everything. The whole city.'

'Where are the soldiers?' cried Gideon. 'They were here earlier.'

'Gone. It's too late. We're all on our own now.'

A sound like thunder split the air.

'That's a musket,' Samuel shouted. 'Run!'

Screams followed him and Gideon as they charged away from the crowd. A second musket round blasted behind them, then other people running away overtook them.

Samuel didn't even know what was happening until afterwards, it was over so quickly. He tumbled over the cobbles, arms and knees scraping the ground, his face grazed. Nobody stopped, least of all those who had sent him flying. Only Gideon came back when he saw Samuel trying to get up off the cobbles.

'Are you hurt?' the younger boy asked, grabbing at Samuel's tunic. 'Can you stand up?'

'Let's get out of here,' Samuel said gruffly, gritting his teeth as the pain all over his body turned into a hot, glowing feeling. 'I know the back way around. We'll go that way.' He pushed himself up.

Samuel herded Gideon into the nearest alley as more people fled past them and another musket went off. For once, the darkness of the passage felt safer, its emptiness not a threat.

'We can take the back streets and alleyways until we're on the other side of the fighting, then join back up with the main street,' Samuel explained as they passed through the dark alleys at an echoing trot.

'What about Catherine?' said Gideon.

Samuel smiled, though in the darkness he knew Gideon wouldn't see it. 'Who do you think taught me how to find my way around this labyrinth? She knows every twist and turn of every street and alley in the city.'

'I wish I did,' Gideon muttered.

Samuel knew exactly where they were. The streets became narrower, the alleys darker, the buildings older, the houses more decrepit. 'Turn right here.'

A door banged sharply behind them. Gideon jumped. Samuel felt his own heart race, ready to power another escape at high speed. 'Just the wind.'

'Why haven't people shut their doors?'

'Why would they?' Sam said as he guided Gideon into another deserted passage. 'People round here have nothing to steal.'

In the dim light from the moon he knew Gideon wouldn't see the crumbling walls of rotting clapboard that held the crooked houses together. In the bitter stink of smoke he wouldn't smell the muck and filth of the untended, unwashed streets. And in its desertedness, he wouldn't see how this part of the city was usually so crowded with the poor, the sick and the old.

Gideon started to cough. 'The smoke's getting thicker.'

'We're downwind of the fire here. We'll be out of it in a moment.' But as the smoke blew across the face of the moon, it also made it harder for Samuel to spot the right turnings. 'On the other side of this courtyard up here is the alley that takes us onto Cheapside.'

He led the way into the courtyard. They were halfway across when he stopped.

'Why are we stopping?' said Gideon.

'It's gone.'

'What's gone?'

'The alley.'

'What do you mean? How can it be gone?'

'Look!' Samuel pointed.

He couldn't remember how long it had been since he had last run through here with Catherine. A month, perhaps. In the meantime the owner of the stables next to the alley had extended it and built an extra stall for another horse.

The alley no longer existed.

'Come on,' he said decisively, trying to make up for the sudden lack of confidence he was now feeling. 'We'll find another way around.'

Gideon followed him, and didn't question why they were running again.

Outside the courtyard Samuel stopped. In his mind's eye this route had been daylit, full of people, the street and passages easy to recognise. Now all he could see was the darkness, and the smoke roiling through it.

'This way,' he said, but even as he said he realised he wasn't sure.

Down streets, round corners, through alleyways, Samuel and Gideon ran. When Samuel started gasping for air he knew he couldn't run from the truth any more. Smoke swirled in all directions, as dense as fog. The narrow passages channelled wind left and right. Though he had slowed to catch his breath, they were both inhaling smoke. Gideon began to cough.

'Cover your mouth with your sleeve,' Samuel said hoarsely, his voice strained by the smoke.

He had no idea where they were, and worse, he didn't even know which direction to head in. The tall buildings seemed to close in, smother him and Gideon in shadow.

For a moment Samuel thought the only thing that would point the way was the fire. But he knew if they got close to that again they would probably never get out of this maze.

Gideon grabbed Samuel's tunic. 'Sam, what's that?'

Samuel didn't need to see Gideon pointing into the darkness to see what he meant. Instantly he felt somewhat lighter, the feelings of despair no longer crushing his shoulders.

Floating in the grey gloom up ahead, where the smoke was even thicker, the flickering yellow light looked like a halo. 'It's a lantern!' Samuel cried.

He couldn't make out whether the person holding it was coming towards them or heading away. Gideon clearly thought the latter.

'Wait for us!' he shouted into the murk.

Together they ran towards the light.

'Help!' Gideon called after its bearer.

But he or she didn't get any further away.

As they reached the lantern's light Samuel saw the woman holding it. She was wearing a long black dress and a woollen shawl with a ragged fringe over her head and shoulders. She was bent over, trying to push a large wooden chest over the cobbles, down the street and out of the smoke.

'Miss,' Samuel called to her, but when she didn't turn he stopped his sleeve muffling his mouth and called again. 'Leave it, miss!'

Only when he and Gideon came up beside her did Samuel see that the woman wasn't bending over the chest. She was slumped over it, and the lantern was simply hanging from her fingers.

Gideon gasped, then staggered back against the nearest house, his chest suddenly full of smoke. Bent double, he started to retch—whether from the taste of smoke or what he had just seen, Samuel didn't know.

Slowly, his hand shaking, Samuel reached out and pulled the dead woman's shawl down so that it covered her face and her half-open eyes.

Then he went over to the younger boy, floundering in the smoke as every breath made him choke. Samuel grabbed him, steadied him, then held his sleeve up to Gideon's red nose and mouth.

'We've got to get out of this smoke,' Samuel told him calmly. 'If we don't, we're going to die here just like her.'

Chapter 21

Samuel approached the dead woman again, just as slowly as he had the first time. His hands weren't shaking, however, when he reached out.

'What are you doing?' said Gideon, the smoke in his throat turning his voice into a hiss.

'We need this more than she does,' Samuel said flatly. He began prising the woman's fingers free of the lantern. They weren't stiff. She could have just been asleep. But Samuel knew she wasn't. He had seen that empty look in her half-open eyes.

'There isn't much oil left,' he told Gideon, lifting the lantern up above their heads. 'Let's make the most of it.'

As he started off in the direction the woman had been going, Samuel heard Gideon whisper something to the woman, perhaps thinking Samuel wouldn't hear over the wind. 'Thank you.'

At the next junction Samuel stopped running to read the names of the little lanes and the passages leading off them.

'I've never heard of any of these streets,' Gideon said.

Samuel grunted. 'Neither have I.'

'Does Catherine know the way better than we do?'

Samuel just nodded.

'Well, what if she gets to St Paul's first, then? She won't know we're lost.'

'She'll wait for us. Let's go this way.'

'Won't she come and look for us?' Gideon asked breathlessly as they ran.

'I'll get us out of here, Gideon. I promise.'

The yellow flame of the lantern flickered, the light dimming before flaring up again. Samuel guessed they only had a few minutes' worth of oil left.

A sound from the darkness rent the air, a sound of life, a not unwelcome noise. It was the bark of a dog, a big one.

'Did you hear that?' He stopped Gideon.

Before Gideon could reply, another bark came out of the shadows, then another. Not just one dog, but two, and both very much alive.

'People!' Gideon cried.

The dogs kept barking as Samuel homed in on where the sound was coming from. He followed the sound into a passage, into a courtyard.

When the dogs saw him and Gideon they started leaping up, straining on the ropes that tied their necks to their kennel.

But there were no people around.

'How could they just leave them tied up?' Gideon said, heading straight for them. 'They'll die.'

'Careful, they might bite,' Samuel warned.

The dogs stopped leaping about as Gideon reached them and lay down in the dirt, chins on the ground, big eyes rolling up to look at the boy. Both dogs started whimpering.

Gideon petted one then the other on the head. 'Help me get the knots undone.'

Samuel looked around, in case someone was still around, but it looked as if the dogs had indeed been abandoned. The dogs panted and wagged their tails as Gideon struggled to pick the first knot apart.

As he headed over to help, Samuel had an idea.

'Let me,' he said. 'When I loosen the other end, keep hold of the dog. They're smart and they'll run in the opposite direction to the fire. They'll help us get out of here.'

Gideon grabbed the dog by its flank, making a fuss of the animal whilst making sure it wouldn't get away.

Unfortunately the dog had other ideas. It knew the moment it was free. Bowling Gideon over, it broke into a run immediately and bounded out of the courtyard.

'Wait!' Gideon shouted after it, scrabbling to his feet to chase after it.

By the time he got up, the dog had disappeared.

'We can't lose this one,' Samuel said as he worked the other knot open. He wound the rope around his wrist a couple of times as he did so.

With its mate free, the other dog had started jumping and straining and barking again. 'Just wait a moment!' Samuel snapped.

Gideon tried to pacify the beast, but it wasn't interested. It pulled the rope around Samuel's wrist taut. He winced as the tightening coil burnt his skin.

Then the knot came loose. Samuel took firm hold of the rope. The dog was strong. Samuel tripped forward a few steps before he matched the panting dog's pace.

'Come on!' he called to Gideon as the dog dragged him past the younger boy.

The dog hurtled out of the courtyard, barking as it went. Samuel tried to rein it back a bit, in case Gideon couldn't keep up, but glancing over his shoulder he saw Gideon belting after them.

The light from the lantern in Samuel's hand ebbed and swelled, but got ever dimmer. He knew it would go out completely at any moment.

Suddenly he lost his grip on the rope. He grabbed at it as the last of the rough cord snaked out of his grasp, searing his palm as it went.

The dog did not slow down. In fact, without Samuel holding it back, it quickly became uncatchable.

'No!' cried Gideon. 'Come back!'

Samuel didn't slow down either. 'Keep running! We can still follow it until it goes out of sight.'

That wasn't long. When the last of its barks vanished into the distance, Samuel and Gideon slowed, absolutely exhausted and gasping for air.

'I can't run any more,' Gideon said.

'It doesn't matter,' Samuel replied. 'Take a deep breath. Go on.'

'I am!'

'But it isn't making us cough.'

It took Gideon a second to realise what Samuel was getting at. 'We're out of the smoke! The dogs led us to safety. Thank you!' He shouted his gratitude this time. 'They earned their freedom.'

Samuel couldn't help himself from laughing. Gideon joined in.

Samuel felt his heart slowing back down to normal. He swallowed, his mouth dry. The first thing he wanted to do after meeting up with Catherine was drink a cup of water.

Then the lantern stopped flickering and the light slowly dimmed to a faint glow.

'We're not safe yet,' Samuel said. 'I still have no idea where we are.'

He shook the lantern, trying to make it last a little longer, but it was no use. The last thing he saw before the darkness of the city closed in on them again was Gideon's face, no longer laughing and smiling but afraid again.

Samuel threw the lantern away angrily. It clattered over the cobbles. 'If I could see St Paul's over the rooftops I'd know exactly where we are and exactly how to get us there!'

'Wait, Sam. That's it!'

'What is?'

'Using St Paul's to find our way there.'

'How?'

Gideon chuckled. 'You must be a really bad thief.'

Samuel was reminded of something Wilf had said to him a long time ago. Then it came to him, what Gideon was suggesting.

'I'm going to break into one of the houses and go up to the roof,' Samuel said.

'That's it!'

In the darkness Samuel could picture Gideon's grin.

The first door Samuel tried was locked. The second creaked inwards when he leant on it.

'Wait here,' he told Gideon.

'No, I'm coming with you,' Gideon said firmly. 'I want to know what it feels like to be a thief.'

Samuel snorted with laughter as he fumbled and stumbled his way into the house. Without even the faint moonlight from outside, the hall and the staircase were hidden in a blanket of pitch darkness. He found the bottom of the stairs when he tried to walk forwards and tripped over the bottom step. The next few steps broke his fall.

'Up here,' he said.

He crawled up speedily on all fours. A dim glimmer of moonlight shone through open shutters on the next floor, lighting the rest of the way up.

'I'm really not a very good thief, it's true,' he said as they went.

'Well, if you're going to be bad at something, that's a good thing to be bad at, I suppose. I'm bad at geometry.'

'What's geometry?'

'Good question!'

Samuel chuckled.

They reached a garret room built into the attic, the sloping sides of the roof reaching a point over their heads. Two dormer windows opened out from either side, weak light shining through the gaps between the shutters.

Gideon went to one and Samuel the other. As he flung the shutters wide open, Samuel saw St Paul's looking more magnificent than he had ever seen it before as it towered over all of the houses, dwarfing even the tallest. His heart sped up at the sight of its lead roof, usually a grey-white mottled colour, shining like a beacon only four or five streets away.

'We're almost there!' he cried jubilantly. 'I know where we are!'

Gideon didn't acknowledge him right away, then finally in a distant quiet voice said, 'Sam, come and look at this.'

Of course Samuel already knew what was making the roof of St Paul's shine like that. He joined Gideon at the other window, and this vision made his heart race even faster.

The fire had followed them. The actual word that came to Samuel's mind was *chased*. A curtain of flame had descended over the city, and Samuel had to move his head left or right to see the ends of it. He had watched it the previous day from the church tower at St Clement's, but since then the fire had spread further and faster than he could have possibly imagined.

He patted a mesmerised Gideon on the shoulder. 'Come on,' he said. 'Let's get out of this city before it burns down around our ears.'

Going down they both took the steps two at a time.

Chapter 22

By the time they reached the lich gate that led into the courtyard of St Paul's, both Samuel and Gideon were breathless again. They slowed to wait behind others heading into the cathedral's grounds. They had already overtaken slow groups and even slower individuals.

When they got past the wall and into the yard, they both stopped, until someone from behind nudged them forward and out of the way.

'There must be hundreds,' said Gideon.

'Perhaps thousands,' said Samuel.

He had never seen the place so busy. Services at the towering cathedral never attracted so many. Every inch of the yard seemed covered by someone sitting, lying, slumping, or where there wasn't enough room to rest, just standing.

'No room, no room,' said a toothless old man in tatty clothes who was rocking back and forth on his heels.

'It's going to take until morning to find a way through all these people,' said Gideon.

Samuel pointed towards people standing. Some were milling forward. 'We'll follow them as far as we can.'

He and Gideon started picking their way through the crowd.

'I had an idea a lot of people would come here,' Samuel said as he tried to avoid stepping on sleeping people wrapped in blankets.

'I'm glad Cathy told us exactly where to meet her,' said Gideon.

Samuel nodded. 'We'd never find her amongst all these people.'

He had expected a lot of people to come here, but he hadn't expected quite so many. It was as though everyone who lived between here and Pudding Lane had flocked here for safety. Exhausted faces of the sleepless and the terrified peered up at Samuel, lit only by moonlight or the occasional lantern.

An eerie silence hung over the courtyard. Hardly anyone they passed was talking to anyone else, and when they did they spoke in whispers. Everyone else huddled in the darkness without speaking, without moving, as if they weren't even there.

'Why did they all come here?' Gideon wondered, whispering himself.

'Perhaps they think this place is too big to burn.'

Gideon looked up at the cathedral. 'It will, though, won't it? They're not safe here.'

Samuel knew he didn't need to answer that.

Following others and threading through whatever gaps people left between them brought Samuel and Gideon to the buttressed wall of the cathedral. Some people had erected little tents against it, but it smelt like most were using it as a privy.

As Samuel followed the wall to the front of the building, it still seemed too strong, too safe, too cold to catch fire.

Samuel couldn't see Catherine on the steps that led up to the porticoed entrance. More people sat and lay on them, leaving only a narrow path. Samuel started up. Gideon followed closely.

A man stood in the middle of the crowd, pointing and shouting. 'Look! With your own eyes, look! No man is safe here! God Himself will not save you. Everyone must leave. Look! The storm is coming.'

Nobody except Samuel and Gideon listened to him. Samuel looked back and from here he could see the fire over the rooftops. It did indeed look like a great orange thunderstorm, great churning clouds lit from within, rolling across the dark horizon. It sounded like a thunderstorm too.

'Can you see her?' Samuel asked Gideon, trying to get his attention back off the inferno.

'What if she got here first and thought we hadn't waited for her?'

'No. She knows we would wait.'

But there was no sign of her beneath the columns at the top of the steps either.

'Perhaps she got caught up like we did and hasn't arrived yet,' Samuel said, but something about that felt wrong.

'Perhaps there wasn't room on the steps when she got here and she went inside,' Gideon suggested.

Samuel nodded, grasping the idea as the only good explanation. 'Perhaps she thought we had gone inside and went to look for us. You wait here and I'll go in and look. Don't move. I can't search for both of you.'

Gideon nodded.

Samuel pushed through the crowd and entered the transept. The cathedral was the tallest building in the city, its peaked roof almost piercing the heavens. But today it felt smaller.

Inside there were just as many people as there were outside. Every pew was occupied, and every aisle and corner had someone sitting or kneeling in it. A murmur of hundreds of whispered prayers filled the air above Samuel's head. Somewhere someone was crying.

Jostled, elbowed and pushed, Samuel found himself herded further inside, into the nave. He pushed back, grabbing at people as they grabbed at him.

'Cathy!' he called, then more desperately, 'Catherine!'

He looked and listened for a response, but no heads turned, no arms waved, no voices called back. Samuel felt something sink inside his chest.

He hurried back to the entrance as fast as he could.

Just before he got to the doors, Gideon shoved his way through them.

'What is it?' Samuel said hopefully. 'Have you found her?'

The other boy couldn't seem to find the words, just shook his head.

Samuel went out into the night again, and saw who Gideon had seen. But it wasn't Catherine who had just reached the top of the steps.

'Good morning, Sam,' said Uncle Jack.

199

Chapter 23

'Where's Catherine?' Samuel demanded.

'She's safe,' said Uncle Jack, in as pleasant a voice as Samuel had ever heard him use. Then he added, not quite so pleasantly, 'For now.'

'Let her go!' Gideon cried.

Uncle Jack ignored him and continued to stare at Samuel. 'Walk with me towards the gate.'

'No,' Samuel said immediately. He knew if he had thought about it another second he would not have been brave enough to say it.

Uncle Jack's eyebrows rose in surprise. He looked Samuel up and down as if he had never seen him before. Then he shrugged, turned round and started down the steps alone. Samuel and Gideon swapped anxious glances.

'I will tell Catherine you said farewell,' Uncle Jack called back to them as he descended.

Samuel looked at Gideon again, bobbed his head to the side apologetically, then headed after Uncle Jack. 'Wait.'

'No time for that,' Uncle Jack said. 'We have much to discuss before we reach the gate, don't we?'

Samuel didn't know whether Catherine would be at the gate. He doubted it. So long as they were inside the yard, though, Jack wouldn't try anything. Heading this way, the gate didn't seem as far from the cathedral steps as it had when he and Gideon arrived.

'Don't follow him!' Gideon hissed at his back.

'Gideon, wait here,' Samuel said.

'No, he will come too,' Uncle Jack said. 'And that is not something I am willing to discuss.'

Gideon glared at Samuel, mouthing words and jabbing his finger at Uncle Jack's back. Samuel didn't understand what he was trying to say and simply mouthed the word, 'Please.'

People in the crowd shifted out of Uncle Jack's way. He swung his stick out ahead of him to make sure of it.

'Catherine told me all about your little plan,' he explained as they went.

'Only because you forced her to,' Samuel guessed.

Uncle Jack shrugged again. 'You should have learnt by now that you can't trick a trickster. I will never put myself in a position where you can fool me again, Samuel.'

'Where is she?' he tried once more.

'So long as you and Gideon keep walking I will take you right to her. Then we shall leave the city together.

That is what I propose. That part of the plan hasn't changed. You and Catherine are perfectly free to come with us when we take Gideon back to his parents, if you are so worried about him, but neither of you will receive a share in the reward. After that, we all go our separate ways.'

If that had really been Uncle Jack's plan, Samuel might have gone along with it. But all Uncle Jack wanted was Gideon. Samuel knew he would say anything to get the boy within Mr Morley's grasp. Samuel and Catherine would only get in the way.

Uncle Jack slowed to a halt and turned to face them, tipping his head back so they could see his eyes under the shadow of his hat.

Gideon and Samuel staggered to a halt just out of his reach.

'I shall wait at the gate whilst you find a way to convince Gideon,' he said, gesturing behind himself with a gloved thumb.

'You will be waiting a long time,' Gideon snarled.

Uncle Jack continued to ignore him. 'Don't take too long, Sam. Catherine's waiting in a house nearby. She's safe for now.' He looked over their heads, towards the burning rooftops in the distance, and frowned. 'But the fire's getting closer all the time.'

With that he turned and hobbled away.

Samuel stayed where he was, watching Uncle Jack go. They were surrounded by people, but that didn't make Samuel feel any safer. He was thinking of the people surrounding Catherine.

Gideon began tugging at Samuel's tunic. 'Don't listen to him, Sam. He's lying. You and Catherine know too much. He will never let you go.'

'I know,' said Samuel, making calming patting gestures with his hand. 'But listen, he's not going to hurt you. I believe that.'

'I don't!'

'Your father will pay him whatever he demands for your release, won't he?'

'Of course!'

'Then he can't hurt you, can he?'

'But Catherine overheard them. That's not what he said.'

'Only if your father won't pay. Which you know he will. If you think about it, it's in Jack's interests to protect you.'

Gideon let out a disbelieving laugh.

'Please, Gideon,' Samuel went on. 'I'm begging you. I won't leave you, I promise you that. But I need you to go along with him for now. He'll lead me right to Cathy. We'll find a way to escape together, you and me and Cathy.'

Gideon looked towards the gate. So did Samuel. He could see Uncle Jack leaning against the wall, a glowing pipe in his hand. Apart from lifting it to his lips and then lowering it again, he didn't move at all.

'I know I can't force you to do this for her, Gideon,' Samuel said. 'It has to be your decision.'

'This is what she did for me,' said Gideon. 'That was really quite brave of her, wasn't it?'

'Yes.'

'She didn't know she might get trapped, did she?'

'Perhaps she did. But perhaps she did it anyway.'

Gideon glanced back at him, the wind blowing the long tousles of his wig away from his face and revealing the set expression of someone who had made up his mind to do the right thing. 'Very brave, then,' Gideon decided.

Samuel nodded. 'So, which way are you walking?'

'This way,' Gideon said firmly, and he pushed past, leading the way towards the lich gate.

Samuel took a deep breath and followed.

'Don't leave me alone with him, Sam,' Gideon said.

'I won't.'

Samuel buried the sudden fear that had struck him, the idea that Uncle Jack didn't actually need Catherine to be waiting for them at the house, so long as Samuel believed she would be there. He didn't know what he would do then.

When Uncle Jack saw them coming he didn't wait for them to reach him. He headed out into the street. He was halfway towards the next corner before they caught up with him.

'Good boy,' he said without looking at Samuel.

'How far is it?' Samuel asked.

'Not far.'

'If you've hurt her, I'll…' He trailed off.

'You'll what?' Now he looked at Samuel.

Samuel didn't have the words to finish the sentence. None of them seemed strong enough.

Uncle Jack chuckled. 'I haven't hurt her, you ridiculous child. I'm not a monster.'

Samuel did have the words to respond to that, but he quickly thought better of using them.

They walked, away from St Paul's, away from people, into dark, abandoned streets. They went in silence.

Chapter 24

Catherine couldn't move, couldn't see and could hardly breathe either. Mr Morley had tied the cords around her wrists and her ankles so tightly that her fingers and toes prickled with pins and needles. Though the cord covering her eyes also covered her ears she could hear herself snorting to breathe. The gag in her mouth tasted like it had been used to clean the floor.

She knew someone else was in the room with her. Every now and then she heard a floorboard creak loudly right behind her. She hoped it was Wilf. She was afraid it was Mr Morley.

Trapped in the darkness of her binding, she lost track of time. She had no idea how long she had been here now. But she knew she was bait for Samuel. She knew he would come for her. She had to save him.

She let out a groan through her gag.

Nobody responded, so she let out another groan and rocked in her chair.

After she did this a third time, rocking more violently on this occasion, she heard the floorboard creak and footsteps leave the room.

She listened to them on the stairs, going down. So wherever she was, she was upstairs. Then two sets of feet came back up.

Someone wrenched the gag from her mouth so forcefully that her head snapped back and hit the top of the chair. She ignored the pain.

'What?' rasped Mr Morley's voice.

'I need to go,' Catherine said.

Mr Morley just laughed. 'You're not going anywhere, my girl. Not until Jack gets back, anyway.'

'No, I need to *go*.'

She heard a boy's whisper. So it had been Wilf guarding her, after all.

'No, I don't think so,' Mr Morley said.

'Please!' she cried.

'No. You can hold it until Jack gets back. I don't imagine he'll be much longer.'

'I'm desperate! Please!'

He laughed again. 'You're desperate to escape, I know. Now open your mouth or I'll open it again for you.'

Catherine remembered him pulling her hair to make her cry out when he first put the gag in. Her scalp still felt scalded. But she kept her mouth shut and shook her head.

'There's a privy in the yard,' Wilf said. 'It backs onto the next house. There's no way she could escape.'

Mr Morley paused to consider his words. 'Undo her feet but tie her hands in front of her instead.' Then to Catherine he said, 'Open your mouth, or you don't go anywhere. There'll be no shouting for help.'

She relented and he roughly forced the cloth back into her mouth.

'Don't let her out of your sight for a moment,' Mr Morley told Wilf. 'If she tries to escape I'll tie you to the other chair, and there won't be nobody coming to rescue you.'

She heard his feet head downstairs.

Then Wilf removed the cloth from her face. Even the light from the lantern seemed bright after sitting in the dark and she squeezed her eyes against the glare.

Wilf undid the cords from her hands and feet. As her eyes grew accustomed to the light she looked for a sign of hope, a sign that Wilf would help her. But as he grabbed her wrists and tied them again in front of her, his expression was blank and he didn't look at her.

'Come on,' he said wearily.

Wilf led her down the stairs, past the room where Mr Morley sat with Mr Boyle, smoking pipes. Wilf took her outside and gestured to the rickety wooden lean-to.

'There,' he said. 'Hurry up.'

Catherine went in and closed the door, but she could still see Wilf through the empty knots in the wood. The worst thing about the gag now was not the taste but the fact that she had to breathe through her nose. The stink from below the privy was enough to make her feel ill. Catherine waited in there for as long as she could stand it.

Wilf had been right that there was no escape from out here. That left only one slim possibility. Before she let him lead her back inside she looked up at the house. Two floors above this one, a dormer window in the roof.

Wilf led her back up the stairs. As they reached the first landing she took several deep breaths through her nose. This was her only chance.

Throwing all her weight into him, she charged into Wilf's back. Caught unexpectedly he tumbled into the room, knocking over the lantern. They were plunged into darkness.

Catherine steadied herself first. She turned and bolted for the stairs. She pounded up them, two steps at a time, sometimes three.

'Help!' Wilf cried from below.

But Catherine was already heading up the final staircase to the garret by the time she heard the cacophony of Mr Morley and Mr Boyle in pursuit.

She ran to the shutters in the dormer window and threw them open. Firelight flooded the room with a blood-red glow. The fire was only a couple of streets away now.

Hard as it was with bound hands, Catherine climbed up into the window frame then lowered herself onto the roof. As soon as her clog touched a slate it slipped out of place, sliding off the roof and smashing on the cobbles below. She held on to the window frame, heart thundering.

Catherine hated heights at the best of times, but the fear of what was coming up behind her evaporated the fear of what lay below. Dropping to a crouch she scurried across the rooftop. A few more slates slipped, but she moved so fast that they didn't take her with them.

'Get out after her!'

She heard Mr Morley's bark and glanced back. Wilf was climbing out of the window.

'Boyle, get down to the street in case she finds a way down.' Mr Morley and Mr Boyle did not follow Wilf out onto the roof.

The gale suddenly accelerated and almost sent Catherine flying. She needed to find a way down before Mr Morley and Mr Boyle reached the front door.

As she crawled from roof to roof she saw the houses that backed onto this street were not as tall. So she dropped down onto one of them, dangling by her fingertips as long as possible so that she didn't have far to fall.

She heard more slates slipping and smashing. Wilf was getting closer.

Edging to the side of the next roof, looking for a lean-to or a privy to drop down onto, she caught sight of the lantern coming along the street.

People, she thought. They would help her.

She reached up and finally tugged the gag from her mouth. It hadn't seemed that important before. But just as she was about to call for help she saw who her would-be rescuers were.

It was Uncle Jack, and with him were Samuel and Gideon.

Catherine felt a great strength rise inside her. She felt like she could shout down a storm.

'Samuel!' she bellowed. 'Stop! It's a trap!'

Chapter 25

Samuel, Gideon and Uncle Jack all froze when they heard the voice. Uncle Jack spun as fast as his leg would let him, searching for Catherine. Samuel spotted her first, clambering over the rooftops above them.

Uncle Jack snapped a look at Samuel, then followed his gaze up to Catherine. Looking back at Uncle Jack, Samuel saw his face crease into a smile. He felt anger rise inside him.

Uncle Jack lunged for Gideon, ready to grab him by the neck. But Samuel was too fast for him. He yanked Gideon out of Uncle Jack's reach and stuck out his foot. Uncle Jack lurched forwards, wooden leg first, right into Samuel's foot. The pain of the hard wood striking Samuel's shin felt like a red hot poker. Samuel stumbled backwards, but didn't fall. Uncle Jack, on the other hand, lost his balance completely. He fell hard onto the cobbles with a furious cry. His hat and stick went flying. The lantern smashed on the ground.

'Run!' Samuel shouted to a bewildered Gideon.

Gideon didn't need telling twice.

'Not that way!' Catherine shouted down.

Samuel grabbed Gideon by the tunic and spun him around. He gave him a push in the other direction, then shot a look at the sprawling Uncle Jack. The glare Uncle Jack gave him back confirmed Samuel's message had got through. It wasn't just a look he had wanted to give Uncle Jack, it was a warning.

Samuel kicked Uncle Jack's stick further out of reach then he ran too, leaving Uncle Jack to pull himself over the cobbles.

Samuel and Gideon ran parallel to the terrace of houses that Catherine was scrambling across. Samuel glanced at her frequently to make sure she could keep up.

They soon reached the end of the terrace. Catherine had nowhere left to go but down or back the way she had come. Her dark shape appeared against the moonlit cloud as she peered over the eaves.

'There's no way down,' she cried.

'Jump!' Samuel called to her.

'I can't! It's too far.'

'We'll catch you,' Gideon shouted, lifting his arms up as if to prove it.

'Yes, we'll catch you!' Samuel echoed, reaching for her too.

Catherine disappeared for a moment, and when she reappeared she came feet first, lowering herself as quickly as she could. Quicker than was safe, thought Samuel.

'Get ready! Quick! Wilf's coming!' she said.

Samuel spotted the other dark shadow climbing across the rooftops. Only two houses away now.

'We're ready!' he told her, stretching out his arms and bending his knees, ready to take the impact. 'Come on!'

Catherine slipped her other leg over the side and then, without its support, fell until only her fingers still clung to the guttering.

Samuel could hear her terrified breathing over the wind. He couldn't breathe at all.

'Come on!' Gideon said.

Wilf loomed up above Catherine.

She didn't get the chance to let go in her own time. The piece of wood bearing her whole body weight suddenly cracked away from the house. She fell with a sharp cry.

Samuel braced in the fraction of a second it took for Catherine to land on top of them. She knocked Gideon sideways and tumbled Samuel onto his back. All the breath blasted out of him as he hit the cobbles. His vision went momentarily black with the pain. It felt like the cobbles had slammed into him, not the other way around.

When he opened his eyes again Catherine was climbing off him, helped by Gideon. Samuel picked himself up and Catherine threw her arms around him. The pain vanished. He hugged her back.

Not to be left out, Gideon wrapped his arms around both of them.

Above them, Wilf looked down. He could pounce, Samuel knew, but he didn't, and when he next looked up, Wilf had vanished.

'I knew you'd come,' said Catherine.

'I knew you'd know,' Samuel replied, smiling.

For a moment they just looked at each other.

Then Gideon suddenly drew back. 'Oh no! Look!'

'No!' Samuel said under his breath.

Coming along the street towards them was Uncle Jack, his stick arcing in quick strides ahead of him. His hat was gone, and his lank hair flew in the wind like dancing fire itself.

'Run!' Samuel cried. He clapped a hand on Gideon's back and grabbed Catherine's hand.

They ran around the corner and onto the next street.

'We can't go this way,' Catherine said as they ran.

'We have to,' said Samuel. 'It's the only way.'

'He's herding us towards the fire. We'll be trapped.'

Samuel feared she was right. 'We'll find a way around. We have to.'

They followed the street around a bend, and all of them scuffed to a stop. Samuel could feel the heat of the houses burning at the other end of the lane from here. Red-hot embers churned out of the smoke like a blizzard of burning snow.

'We have to go back!' cried Gideon.

They got back to the corner in time to see Uncle Jack come around the last one.

'We're only one street away from the river,' Samuel said quickly. 'It's right on the other side of these warehouses. Can you see that alley?' He pointed towards the other end of the lane, towards the fire. 'That will lead us down to the water's edge. Catherine, am I wrong?'

She shook her head. 'You're not.'

'We've got to cover our heads. Come on.'

'Sam, I'm scared,' said Gideon.

Samuel loosened his tunic and pulled it up over his ears like a hood. He gave the younger boy a smile. 'You do trust me, don't you?'

Gideon began to undo his top buttons.

Uncle Jack was gaining on them. Not even on Pudding Lane had Samuel and Catherine got this close to the flames. The heat seemed to steal the breath from Samuel's lungs. It was so hot he was sure his clothes must actually be on fire. He felt his skin start to blister.

But when they reached the turning into the alley that led down to the riverbank, things got much, much worse.

Gideon started saying 'No. No!' repeatedly.

Even Catherine was looking at Samuel and shaking her head.

Buildings on both side of the alley were on fire. Flames lapped up the walls. Tongues of fire licked at the air between the buildings, flicking in the wind like whips being cracked. The building at the far end had a jettied upper storey. This too was burning.

Their escape route looked like a tunnel of fire.

'I can see the river,' Samuel croaked, as smoke churned around them. 'Look! It's only a short run. We can make it.' Though even as he said it, he wasn't sure if it really was water he could see, or simply the infernal, unbearable heat making the air shimmer.

'Don't do it!' a voice called from behind them.

They turned to see Uncle Jack. He stopped, an arm up to his face. Whether it was the heat keeping him back or he was trying not to scare them by keeping his distance, Samuel wasn't sure. He suspected the latter. That was Uncle Jack's kind of ruse.

'That way lies only certain death,' Uncle Jack went on, creeping forward ever so slowly.

Gideon didn't back away from Uncle Jack. Now the old crook wasn't the thing that terrified him most. Samuel stepped in front of Gideon protectively.

'Come back here,' Uncle Jack implored them, reaching out a hand. 'You'll be safe.'

Even Catherine looked like she was considering it.

'You'll be safe,' Uncle Jack repeated. 'With me.'

And that was when everything changed.

'Samuel, how far is it?' Gideon asked, not taking his eyes off Uncle Jack.

'We can run it in five seconds.'

'Are you both ready to do this?' asked Catherine.

'Yes,' said Gideon.

'Yes,' said Samuel. 'Now!'

Uncle Jack roared. He was close enough to swing his stick at them like a halberd.

Catherine was already running full pelt into the alley, and Samuel shoved Gideon after her, so hard he almost knocked the boy off his feet.

Samuel ran after them both, almost bent over, not looking where he was going, arms cradled over his head. He heard Uncle Jack behind him. Over the roaring flames, the howling gale, the creak and crack of burning timber, he could hear Uncle Jack's cries of fury.

Then Samuel entered the tunnel of fire. He batted away bits of burning wood falling from the jettied upper storey. He could see only his clogs kicking through ashes and embers, sending pieces of black, smoking rubble flying.

Just as he thought the all-enveloping heat was about to consume him completely, Samuel felt suddenly cold.

He didn't stop, kept running, but threw his tunic back from his head. Catherine and Gideon had stopped, faces black and streaming with sweat, mouths gasping for air.

Samuel finally looked back, just in time to see Uncle Jack attempt to run through the tunnel of fire. He made it halfway through before there was an almighty crash. Samuel saw the look on his face. He had never seen Uncle Jack look frightened before.

Uncle Jack was still running when the jettied upper storey collapsed.

Samuel staggered back as a billowing cloud of thick smoke swallowed everything, burning rubble tumbled in every direction and embers bounced across the ground.

Catherine and Gideon were now standing on a narrow wooden wharf that jutted out into the River Thames. Catherine tried to drag Samuel after them.

'Come on, Sam,' she urged.

As the smoke cleared from the alleyway Samuel saw Uncle Jack writhing on the ground. Daring to get closer, Samuel saw why. Uncle Jack's wooden leg was on fire. First he tried slapping at the flames, crying out as the fire seared his palms. Then he gave up, and tore at his breeches until the stump of his knee was exposed. He grabbed the cushioned top of the false limb and pulled it off. He threw the burning leg out of his way, but he was still surrounded by flaming rubble.

'Come on, Sam,' Catherine urged again. 'The rest of the building will collapse any moment.'

'We can't leave him like that,' said Samuel.

As if to emphasise Catherine's point, the roof of the next building suddenly burst inwards, raining burning debris down onto the next wharf. Some fell into the water with a loud hiss.

'We have to go,' said Gideon.

Samuel ignored them and approached Uncle Jack. He couldn't get close enough to help him. Samuel had to shout to him through the flames: 'Where's your stick?'

Uncle Jack finally stopped flailing about and locked eyes with Samuel. Yellow flames reflected in his black pupils. For a moment they just stared at each other.

'Get out of here, you stupid boy,' Uncle Jack said eventually, his voice gruff and weak.

Samuel spotted Uncle Jack's stick then. It was behind him in the alley, broken in two, both parts burning.

He felt Gideon tug at his arm. 'Come on, Sam. We've got to go now.'

Samuel nodded. But as he hurried after Gideon he saw a length of unburned wood lying by the side of the wharf. He grabbed it and tossed it back towards Uncle Jack. He never saw whether Uncle Jack picked it up and used it as a walking stick, or whether Uncle Jack even noticed it at all.

'I can't swim,' Gideon said as they edged further along the wharf, further away from the flames.

'Neither can I,' said Catherine.

'None of us can,' said Samuel. 'I thought there might be a little dinghy we could take.'

'All the boats went hours ago.'

'Then we're trapped!' cried Gideon.

The windswept waters of the river reflected the orange firelight. It looked like the Thames was on fire too.

As he stood watching the water eddy past, Samuel saw a large charred piece of wood float by, just out of reach.

'We're not trapped,' he said.

Catherine must have realised what he was thinking a second later. 'It's the only way.'

'What is?' said Gideon.

Samuel and Catherine ran back along the wharf. Without discussion they both went for the same piece of broken wood, a large unburnt beam shattered at both ends.

'Heave!' Samuel shouted.

They both pulled at the same time. It was so heavy it didn't shift at first. Even when it did start to scrape along the deck Samuel worried it was so heavy it would not float, and might even sink instantly.

Gideon joined them, grabbing the beam near the middle, but Samuel's back still sang with pain by the time they reached the end of the wharf.

'We need to jump in after it right away, before it floats off without us,' he said.

'How deep is it?' Gideon said.

'One way to find out.'

Samuel pushed the end of the beam over the edge. Its weight pulled the rest of the beam after it. As it plunged into the river it shot an almighty splash into the air. Filthy, stinking water drenched the three of them.

Samuel didn't hesitate. As soon as he saw the beam bob to the surface, as if it was as light as a twig, he leapt in. Catherine and Gideon jumped in after him.

After flailing for a moment, each of them hugged their arms around the beam, and then it started carrying them down the river, away from the wharf, away from the fire.

Samuel didn't know what it was that made him turn his head and look back. It was an awesome sight, every building on the banks of the Thames as far as he could see on fire. He could have believed the entire city was on fire when he saw that. The spectacle made him let go for a second, and he slipped beneath the surface.

When he came back up, spluttering, he spat out the foul water and blinked his eyes clear. He could have easily drowned, but for the first time that day he actually felt safe.

He hugged the beam even harder than before and began to kick with his legs.

Several days later

By the time the fire had finally burnt itself out, Samuel, Catherine and Gideon were sitting on top of wooden chests in the back of a merchant's cart. Green fields, ancient woodland and thatched cottages rolled by as the merchant's horses pulled them across the Essex countryside.

A black pall of smoke still hung over London. They had watched it ever since they left from Wapping the previous morning.

'Do you think it looks smaller today?' asked Catherine.

'Perhaps they've finally put it out,' said Gideon.

'Perhaps it just looks smaller because we're further away,' said Samuel.

They reached the outskirts of Brentwood just before lunchtime. The merchant dropped them off at the end of the path that led up to Gideon's parents' house.

Now that they were finally here, Samuel wondered if they shouldn't be. This house was twice the size of the one in London, the one he and Catherine had tried to rob. The house had a beautiful brown thatched roof and thin grey smoke spiralling gently out of a couple of chimneys, one at either end of the building. Glancing at Catherine, he could see she was similarly apprehensive.

'Gideon, are you sure we will be welcome?' he asked.

Gideon stopped in the middle of the path and gave them shocked looks. 'Why wouldn't you be welcome? You saved my life. You're like the big brother and sister I never had.'

Then he ran up to the front door and started hammering.

'Mother! Father! It's me! I'm home!' he cried.

Samuel and Catherine looked at each other and smiled, but Samuel still felt slightly anxious when he heard several pairs of feet rushing to the door.

And then it opened, and Samuel and Catherine found out just how welcome they were.